TROUBLE
AT SILVER PINES INN

GLORIA REPP

Illustrated by Gabriela Dellosso

JOURNEY
B O O K S ™
Greenville, South Carolina

Library of Congress Cataloging-in-Publication Data

Trouble at Silver Pines Inn

Project Editor: Debbie L. Parker
Designed by Duane A. Nichols

© 1998 Journey Books
Published by Bob Jones University Press
Greenville, South Carolina 29614

ISBN 1-57924-000-3

15   14   13   12   11   10   9   8   7   6   5   4   3   2   1

For John and Pearl Sprigg,
who first took me to the Atlantic shore

Books by Gloria Repp

The Secret of the Golden Cowrie
The Stolen Years
Night Flight
A Question of Yams
Noodle Soup
Nothing Daunted
Trouble at Silver Pines Inn

Contents

1

I Told You

Now that it was getting dark, Nick could hardly keep his eyes open. He'd finished his book, and Robbie, curled up in the car's back seat, wouldn't want to talk. He was listening to his cassette player.

How soon would they get to the Inn? A long drive, Mom had said, and he didn't want to pester her with questions. He was almost twelve now, not a little kid.

But there was something he really had to ask. About Grandfather.

Mom had told him and Robbie that this year at the Inn would be different, that Grandfather would be there. He had broken his leg, and Aunt Margo had persuaded him to come stay with her.

Nick had seen Grandfather several years earlier, at a family get-together arranged by Aunt Margo. All he could remember was an old man with angry black eyes.

He slid close to his mother. "I know a broken leg really hurts. Is that why you said Grandfather is being difficult?"

Mom took a deep breath, and he knew she didn't want to answer. She'd never told him much about Grandfather, no matter how many questions he asked.

She drove for a while in silence. Finally she said, "Your grandfather is an angry man, Nicky. He's been that way for years, ever since your daddy died."

"He's got Aunt Margo."

"Yes, but Daddy was his only son. They were very close until Daddy became a Christian. Then everything changed."

"Oh." He'd always wondered about Grandfather, wishing that he lived closer. Maybe things would have been different.

Outside, trees and houses and more trees rushed by, just as they had all day. The road, lit by the car's headlights, seemed to go on forever. He'd given up pretending that the Inn was just beyond that next clump of trees.

Robbie had told him about the Inn, how it was big and old, and how Aunt Margo would wear herself out if Mom didn't help by taking over once a year.

Mom had never let him come before. She always said it was no vacation and he shouldn't miss school anyway. Robbie always said he was too small for the hard work. But this year Mrs. Elliot couldn't stay with him, so Mom had made arrangements with Nick's teacher like she did for Robbie.

I'm eleven now—I can work as hard as Robbie, Nick thought. Mom will be glad she let me come.

He stared out at the dark countryside. What would it feel like to stand at the edge of the Atlantic Ocean? Was it really as big as the books said? His thoughts drifted to the story he'd just finished reading. Pretty clever, the way Shane Hemming had figured out where to find the treasure. You never know what might be buried on a beach . . . He leaned back and closed his eyes.

"Wake up, Short Stuff. I'm not carrying you up those stairs." It was Robbie's voice that jerked him awake, and those were Robbie's strong hands pulling him out of the car.

Cold wind splashed into his face, wet and salty as seawater. He opened his eyes wide. An impossibly tall house loomed above them with light streaming from its open doorway.

A plump figure was hugging Mom, hugging Robbie, hugging him. It was like being enfolded by a pillow, he thought sleepily—a warm, fragrant pillow.

"Nicky, I'm so glad you came too," Aunt Margo said. "Welcome to Silver Pines Inn!" She kept a hand on his shoulder as he stumbled into the house.

In the darkened hallway, he had a confused impression of many doors and a long flight of stairs to be climbed. Aunt Margo's voice dropped to a whisper. "We'd better not waken Mrs. McHugh." She took his arm. "Up the stairs."

Finally she said, "Here's your room." She turned on a lamp that slanted light across flowered wallpaper, a small bed, an oval rug. "And here's your suitcase. Your mother will be up to see you in a little while."

Nick yawned widely, noticing with satisfaction that the bed was under a window. He yawned again, struggled into his pajamas, and fell shivering into bed. One more effort—to turn out the lamp—and then the room was dark. From where he lay, he could see the limbs of a pine tree and about a million stars. He smiled as he pulled the blankets up to his chin.

Next morning, the first thing that caught his eye was the tree, looming dark against a gray sky. He knelt on his bed to look out. Might be a good tree for climbing. Prickly, maybe, but the branches were well spaced. If he could just get this window open—

Someone knocked sharply on the door. "Better hurry downstairs if you want breakfast," Robbie said.

Nick hurried. He hadn't even caught a glimpse of Grandfather last night. Maybe he'd see him at breakfast.

By the time he reached the kitchen, Mom was pouring her second cup of tea, and Robbie was attacking a pile of pancakes. There was no sign of Grandfather, so he said his own grace and helped himself. Grandfather probably ate breakfast in his room.

Mom picked up her teacup and headed for the sink before Nick had finished eating. Robbie stood up too. "Can't sit around here all day, Short Stuff," he said. Sometimes he sounded like he was eighty years old instead of fifteen.

Mom smiled at them both. "I guess we'd better get started," she said. "There's plenty to do."

Plenty was the word for it, Nick decided as the morning wore on. Aunt Margo had already left, and Mom had organized everything with lists. He wanted to get down to the beach right away, but his jobs were on a list too. Help with dishes. Feed the three cats. Lots of vacuuming and dusting. The vacuum cleaner was an old upright that growled like a living creature, but he could handle it okay.

Robbie had told him the rules. Always roll up the cord to the vacuum cleaner. Shake rugs out the kitchen door. Don't leave equipment lying around. Nick felt as though he were part of a huge, efficient cleaning machine.

He started in the living room, with its big stone fireplace. It faced the ocean, and the distant booming of the surf drew him to the window. Gray, white-tipped waves swept in endless rows toward the strip of beach. Too cold for swimming. But this afternoon he was going to explore that beach.

The Hemming Brothers had discovered pirates' treasure at a beach like this one. His favorite part was the chapter about the hurricane, how it had moved the sand dunes and uncovered a secret cave.

Reluctantly Nick turned back to his vacuuming. He worked his way through the living room and into the dining room. Behind that was the kitchen, and across the hall from the kitchen was a room with its door open. For the man who was supposed to arrive this afternoon? Nick glanced inside while he vacuumed the hall. Blue rug, blue curtains, blue bedspread, and lots of shiny old furniture.

I hope the guy likes blue, he thought. I wonder if he'll be young or old.

The next two rooms were occupied by the woman who was their other guest. She came every fall, Mom said. She was being very quiet, or else she was out somewhere.

A doorbell rang while Nick was sweeping the hearth, and he ran to open the back door. A blond young man dressed in work clothes grinned at him. "Hi, are you the new janitor?"

It took Nick an instant to realize that he still held the broom in one hand. He smiled back. "I sure feel like it."

"Well, I'm Peter," said the man. "My wife and I help Miss Margo with the work around here, so now I know where to find an assistant if I need one."

"Peter, how good of you to stop by!" Mom stepped out of the kitchen, drying her hands on her apron. "I see you've met my son Nicky."

"Sure have, ma'am. I guess Miss Margo has already left?"

"Yes," said Nick's mother. "She wanted to get away early this morning. But come in! Have some coffee and tell me what you and Jackie are doing these days."

Peter smiled, holding up a small plastic bag. "Sure wish I had time, Mrs. Radford. But I just dropped by to fix the hinge on the screen door. Been meaning to, ever since we had that hurricane."

"Hurricane?" said Nick. "Did you have a hurricane around here?"

"Actually, it was the tail end of one," said Peter. "Good thing, or this old house would have blown away. As it was, we lost a bunch of pine trees and part of the beach."

"When was this?" asked Nick's mother.

"Back in September," said Peter. "And I'm still fixing things on this house! Well, the morning's half gone, and I've got to get back to town by noon."

"I understand," Mom said. "Guess I'll see you next Saturday? Bye."

Nick strolled back to the living room. A hurricane! Maybe it had uncovered something interesting on the beach. But first—these chores.

The second-floor hall would be easy to clean, since that's where he and Robbie and Mom were staying, so he left it for last.

He'd do the third floor next. Grandfather's room was up there.

As he bumped the vacuum cleaner up the steps, Nick wondered what to say if Grandfather called to him. But he could see only one door and it was closed, so he plugged in the vacuum and set to work on the dark strip of carpet in the hall.

No sooner had he started than something bumped against the wall beside him. He stopped to listen and heard it again: *Thump-thump. Thump-thump.*

His mother appeared on the stairs, frowning and motioning to him. He turned off the vacuum to see what was the matter.

"I *told* you—" she said in a loud whisper, "don't *vacuum* up here."

"Oh, no! I forgot." He stared at the wall. "Was that Grandfather? Guess I woke him up. I'm sorry!"

"Use the dust mop and the broom." She shook her head at him and disappeared.

He hauled the vacuum cleaner back down the stairs, grabbed a broom, and did a fast job on the dark little hall. The stairs were pretty dusty, so he made himself slow down for them.

The carpet on the second-floor hall wasn't much of a job, but vacuuming it seemed to take forever. He kept waiting to hear an angry thump from Grandfather's room.

At the far end of the hall, he paused to look out a window. From this height he couldn't hear the ocean, but he could see a long way down the beach. A woman in a black skirt moved slowly across the sand, followed by a large black dog. Every once in a while, the woman stopped to poke her stick at something in the dunes. What was she looking for? Nick wondered about that as he went downstairs to shake out his mop.

Robbie was cleaning the hall mirror, so Nick took a detour to ask him about the woman. "That's Mrs. McHugh," said Robbie. "She's in the corner guest rooms. Her dog's pretty old. Hey, are you almost finished? It's time for lunch."

They sat at the kitchen table to eat their peanut butter sandwiches, and Mom explained the rest of the schedule. Afternoons were free time, but they had to be back by 4:30 to help with supper. Evenings were for schoolwork.

Robbie jumped up from the table and hustled his plate and glass into the dishwasher. "I'm going fishing," he announced. He clattered downstairs to the basement closet where the fishing tackle was kept. Nick followed him.

"Can I go fishing with you?"

"Well . . ."

Nick hurried to explain. "I won't really fish or anything. I just want to get out onto the beach, and Mom won't worry if I'm with you."

Robbie shrugged. "Okay, I guess. Be ready in five minutes."

2
Oh, Poor Boy

When Nick asked whether he could go fishing with Robbie, his mother didn't seem to mind. "Wear your red jacket—the one with the hood," she said. "It's winter, remember, and that wind gets awfully cold."

Nick finished his sandwich in three bites and ran to get his red jacket. As soon as he left the veranda, the wind snatched at him, ruffling his hair. He sprinted down the steps to the beach.

A minute later Robbie joined him. "Want to carry something?" He handed Nick a small, battered cooler.

"What's in here?" An afternoon snack wasn't a bad idea, Nick thought.

His brother gave him an annoyed glance. "Nothing's in there, Short Stuff. It's for the fish." He shifted his tackle box impatiently, then turned down the beach toward a pile of rocks. Nick took his time following.

Now the ocean sparkled under pale sunshine, and the waves had turned to blue. He squinted at the horizon. Miles and miles of glittering water stretched as far as he could see. The bright expanse made him feel like shouting.

He swerved down to the water's edge, stamping footprints in the damp, gray sand. The foaming water swished up to his feet, then slid back again. He took deep breaths of the salty air.

Robbie waited for him at the rock pile. The wide line of tumbled rocks extended into the ocean like a pier. On the other side of it, waves lapped at the foot of a cliff.

"What's the matter?" asked Nick.

Robbie shook his head. "Used to be a beach there," he said, frowning at the cliff. It looked as though a giant spoon had scooped away all the sand.

"Peter told us a hurricane came through a while back," Nick said. "And they lost some of the beach."

"Guess that's what happened. Too bad! That was one of my best fishing spots." Robbie turned and started out into the rocks.

"Where're you going?"

"Out here on the jetty," Robbie said. "You can come, but be careful; it's slippery. Leave the cooler there." His long strides took him farther and farther away.

The rocks weren't much bigger than cement blocks, but Nick found that getting over them was awkward. His legs were too short to step across them like Robbie did. Sometimes he jumped from rock to rock, and sometimes he took scrambling little steps that inched him along. Even when he went slowly, he slipped once or twice. He kept an eye on the ocean beside him. The farther out he went, the deeper it got. Waves slapped against the rocks, occasionally splashing up into his face.

When he had almost reached the end of the jetty, he looked back. Maybe from here he could see signs of a cave or a likely spot for hiding treasure. The place where the beach had been washed away didn't look very promising—just an ordinary cliff. But next to it were plenty of sand dunes. From there, the beach stretched smoothly past the Inn, curving around a point of land to his right.

Nick was about to take another cautious step when a star-shaped red kite climbed into the air from somewhere beyond the point. "Look at that kite!"

Robbie glanced up from baiting his hook. "Yeah, I saw a couple of 'em last year."

"Who's flying it?"

"Who knows? I don't usually fish down there."

Nick watched the red star float higher and higher. It was a different sort of kite, with streamers attached. Sometime he'd like to see it up close.

He gazed back over his shoulder at the beach. While Robbie was fishing, he could check out some of those dunes. He turned quickly, missed his footing, and slipped.

This time he went down. He clawed at the slick black rocks, gasping as the icy water soaked through his jeans. Finally he got an arm around one rock and held on with desperate strength.

"Nick!" Robbie dropped his pole and leaped toward him. "I *told* you to be careful."

He leaned down, grabbed Nick's free hand, and pulled him up. "Get back to the Inn as fast as you can—and change, or you'll turn into a block of ice. Guess I'd better . . . " He held tightly to Nick's arm and propelled him along the jetty until the water on either side was only a few inches deep. "Now hurry, or you'll be in big trouble, and me too."

Nick scuttled the rest of the way to the beach on his hands and knees. Then he forced himself to run, in spite of the wet jeans that seemed frozen to his legs. He cast a regretful look at the dunes on his way past. Maybe tomorrow.

He slipped through the back door of the Inn, up the stairs, and into his room. A small gray-striped cat blinked at him from the bed. This was the friendly one, he remembered.

"Hello there," Nick said. "You wouldn't have liked it out on that jetty either."

As soon as he'd changed, he sat down to tickle the soft gray fur under her chin. She was tiny, compared to the other two cats. "You're small for your age, Short Stuff." She closed her eyes, and a rumble started deep in her throat, swelling into a great, rolling purr that seemed impossibly loud for such a little creature.

He hung his jeans in the bathroom to dry, leaving his wet socks and sneakers in the bathtub. On the way back to his room, he paused, looking up the staircase to the third floor. It wouldn't hurt to check on Grandfather. Maybe his door was open now.

Nick set his stockinged feet silently on each step, going just far enough to see down the hall. The door was still closed.

He leaned against the banister. Was Grandfather lying awake in his bed, glaring at the ceiling with his angry black eyes?

He'd read about grandfathers, plenty of times. They were kind and wise. They laughed a lot and told stories. Sometimes they forgot things.

He crept up the last few steps and along the hall. Not a sound came from behind Grandfather's door. Was it dark in there? For a minute he studied the big, old-fashioned keyhole below the glass doorknob, then he stooped to look through it. Yes, dark, like twilight.

An angry-sounding snort made him jump back. Harsh breathing came from the room. It's just Grandfather snoring, he told himself. But the rough, grating sounds seemed to follow as he retreated down the stairs, and he didn't take an easy breath until he reached his own room.

Thinking that he should do some unpacking, he sat down on the bed and gazed at his suitcase. A bird flew past and drew his attention to the window. The tree outside beckoned. It wasn't the tall, skinny kind of pine tree he was used to. This one spread its branches wide—thick, knobby branches, bristling with ragged clumps of pine needles that made it look like a prickly old giant. He'd sure like to climb it. How could he get out there?

The window didn't budge until he banged it loose from layers of paint, but finally he managed to push it upward. Cool, damp air rushed into his room, and with it came the murmuring voice of the sea. The cat perched on the windowsill beside him.

He leaned out as far as he could. Below him was a small roof. That must be the kitchen down there, he decided, trying to remember the layout of the house. Branches from the pine tree reached across the kitchen roof. The biggest one looked dead, but a couple of the others would be fine for climbing.

He glanced up as a small orange car rattled down the long driveway, its headlights cutting twin paths through the dusk. Nick drew back into the window to watch. It stopped behind the Inn, and a tall, red-haired man pulled three suitcases from the car. Must be the new guest. He looked young, but it was hard to tell.

Voices rose from below. Mom was giving the man a warm welcome.

Quietly Nick pulled the window shut. Downstairs might be an interesting place right about now. Just in case things got dull, he took along his Hemming Brothers book.

In the living room, Robbie was feeding sticks to a small fire. "Wondered where you were," he said. "How about bringing me another load of wood? It's stacked outside the kitchen door."

"Sure." He'd forgotten! He was supposed to be helping.

Nick left his book on the sofa and hurried through the dining room to get to the kitchen. A tall, gray-haired lady stood there with his mother, earnestly discussing a menu. Cherry cake. Ham sandwiches. Chocolate éclairs, whatever those were.

On his way back with an armload of wood, he took another look at the woman. Was she the one he'd seen on the beach? Yes. Must be Mrs. McHugh. She didn't have her stick or the dog. Did she keep that dog in her bedroom?

He tripped over something solid and black, dropped two pieces of wood, and caught himself from falling headlong. A big black dog lurched to its feet and eyed him reproachfully.

Mrs. McHugh rushed toward them, her bracelets jingling. "Oh, poor boy, are you all right?" Nick opened his mouth to answer, then closed it. She was kneeling by the dog, patting him all over.

She might as well put a Band-Aid on an elephant, he thought, picking up the wood. It was just a bump.

"I'm sorry—"

But the woman had risen to her feet and was towering over him. "Young man, you'd be well advised to watch where you're going. You could have hurt dear old Chaucer."

"Yes, ma'am," he said. He made a wide circle around the two of them.

Mrs. McHugh followed him into the living room, and he tried to look busy, helping Robbie with the fire. The dog must have come with her, for she directed it to lie down by the fireplace. Out of the corner of his eye he saw her sit on the sofa right next to his book. She picked it up.

She glanced at the cover, then surveyed the living room. "Whose is this?" She sounded as though she had found a murder weapon.

"It's mine, ma'am." Now what?

She fixed her gaze on him. Gray eyes, she had. Sharp as icicles.

"Young man, you shouldn't be reading this nonsense." She glared at the cover; her voice rose. "*The Hemming Brothers Dig for Gold*. Such a waste! Flimsy characters. Insipid plots. My Malcolm always used to say, 'Never fill your mind with junk.' You should be reading some good books. Have you read *Kidnapped*? *Big Red*? *Men of Iron*?"

Nick shook his head, feeling as though he'd failed a test.

She gave the book in her hand a twitch, and for a minute he thought she was going to throw it into the fire. But she dropped it back onto the sofa. "Good for nothing!"

A deep voice spoke from the doorway. "But surely, ma'am, the Hemming Brothers are better than nothing. Consider that many boys his age watch approximately twenty hours of television every week and read only 1.6 books per year."

Mrs. McHugh turned, her eyebrows raised, and the red-haired young man stepped forward. He wore a red plaid suit jacket that lit up the dusky room.

"Forgive me for interrupting," he said. "I'm Archibald Finlay, ma'am. I couldn't help overhearing your conversation."

To Nick's surprise, the old lady inclined her head. "Finlay, is it? Could you possibly have Scots blood in your veins?"

"Yes, indeed. My ancestors belonged to the Clan Farquharson."

"Then we must talk sometime," she said with a smile. "My husband's family comes from Edinburgh."

"Nicky!" Robbie was signaling to him. "Mom wants you in the kitchen." Nick threw a grateful glance at the red-haired man and slipped out of the room.

3
A Likely Spot

After supper, while he was helping to clean up the kitchen, Nick asked his mother about the red-haired man.

"Archibald Finlay finished college just a few years ago," she said. "We just call him Archie. He doesn't have much money—seems to be a rather literary sort. And it sounds like he's getting along fine with Flora McHugh."

Her mouth curved into a mischievous smile. "He'll certainly add a bit of color to tomorrow's Tea."

"Tomorrow's tea? What's that?"

"Every Sunday, Mrs. McHugh puts on an afternoon Tea, with a capital *T*. It's held in her parlor and is quite elegant. We are all expected to attend."

Nick groaned. "Me and Robbie too?"

"Yes," said his mother. "Cheer up. You might even like it."

"What about Grandfather?"

A shadow crossed her face. "No, I'm sure he won't be there."

Nick finished drying the meat platter and set it down, then he asked carefully, "How's he doing, by the way?"

His mother closed her eyes and rubbed the back of her neck. "He's not eating much. He wouldn't even talk to me today."

Nick chewed on his bottom lip. "I guess when I made all that noise . . ."

"No, that wasn't so terrible. Don't worry about it." She sighed. "It's not an accident, you know—your grandfather breaking a leg and our coming here. We've got to pray for him, Nick."

He leaned against the counter, intrigued.

Finally she went on. "I've been asking the Lord to help me love that man." She wiped the counter with quick strokes. "But meanwhile, I don't know how to handle him. The doctor says he's got to exercise or he'll be bedridden for the rest of his life. Old bones get brittle, and muscles atrophy if they aren't used."

Nick could guess what 'atrophy' meant: something bad.

She turned to the sink and began scrubbing it vigorously. "Mrs. McHugh likes to have the kitchen to herself when she cooks for her tea party, so we'd better hurry." Without looking up, she asked, "Have you unpacked yet?"

"No, I—"

"And your teacher said something about a project for school. What's that all about?"

Nick dried the butcher knife while he tried to remember the page of instructions. "Well, instead of doing regular homework, I'm supposed to make two notebooks. One's like a diary—write down the stuff that happens every day. The other is like a scientist's study notebook—write about some living creature I find around here. Robbie's supposed to do one too."

"Have you picked out a subject yet?"

"Not really."

"Better decide soon, so you can get started. I wonder what Robbie's chosen." His mother gave the sink one last swish of her cloth. "There, now we're finished."

On the way upstairs, she said, "Tomorrow's Sunday, remember. Let's get together in my bedroom after breakfast, and we'll listen to one of the sermon tapes I brought. We can sing, too, if you'd like."

"Okay," said Nick. He'd been wondering what they were going to do about church, since Mom couldn't leave the Inn. Maybe after lunch he would go down to the beach.

The next morning when their worship time was over, Nick followed Robbie downstairs. "You going fishing this afternoon?" He glanced outside, hoping it wouldn't rain today. Mom worried now about him getting cold and wet.

"Maybe later," said Robbie. "Guess I'll try the jetty again. But first we're going to Mrs. McHugh's Tea, remember?"

"Oh."

His brother grinned at him. "It's not so bad. She doesn't make us play dumb games, and the food is pretty good."

That afternoon, Mrs. McHugh met them at the door of her parlor with a tray of little sausages wrapped in spicy bread. Nick took one, and after looking around for her dog, sat gingerly in the closest chair.

"Good afternoon, Mrs. McHugh." Archie's voice filled the small room. "Looks like a lavish spread you have here. But I don't see your dog."

Mrs. McHugh smiled. "Chaucer knows his place, Mr. Finlay. He doesn't come to my tea parties."

"Chaucer's his name, eh? One of my favorite poets. A fine old boy."

Nick wasn't sure whether Archie meant the poet or the dog, but Mrs. McHugh didn't seem to mind. She stepped closer to Archie. "Someone gave me a modern translation of *The Canterbury Tales,* but I think it's more beautiful in the Middle English, don't you, Mr. Finlay?"

"Definitely," said Archie.

While the two of them went on talking, Nick surveyed the room. Plump chairs jostled tables that were filled with small framed pictures, painted trays, dried flowers, and oddly shaped pieces of wood. Books were stacked on the floor beside his chair, and under the tables he could see more books. The largest table stood in a corner, covered with trays of food.

"Well, hello there." Archie took two embroidered pillows off a chair next to Nick, added them to a pile of books, and sat down. His tie swung out from his red suit jacket, and Nick eyed it in fascination. He'd never seen a tie with scoops of ice cream painted on it.

"How come you're not eating?" Archie said. "Better catch up with your brother."

Robbie was already at the table, filling his plate with food. "Sure," said Nick. He'd been trying to keep out of Mrs. McHugh's way. Cautiously he approached the table and followed Robbie's example. He found that chocolate éclairs were a kind of pastry filled with custard and topped with chocolate icing; they tasted wonderful. Besides the cherry cake and the ham sandwiches, there were raisin scones, strawberry tarts, a pile of grapes, and cheese cut into little chunks. He took some of everything.

Mrs. McHugh stood to one side, pouring tea. She wore a silvery gray dress with a pearl necklace that made her look like a queen, and every time she lifted the teapot, her silver bracelets clinked. Since there was cocoa, he didn't have to drink tea—he was glad for that.

Half an hour later, Nick caught Robbie's eye and motioned toward the door. "Okay," his brother said, "but she won't like it if we just take off."

Robbie spoke briefly to Mrs. McHugh, and she smiled at them. "Run along, lads," she said. "Thank you for coming."

Mom gave him her "be careful" look as they left, but she didn't say anything, and Nick hurried upstairs to change. He pulled on his still-damp sneakers, just in case, and caught up with Robbie as he went out the back door.

"We've got less than an hour," his brother warned. "We can't be late. There's lots of dishes from the party."

"Okay," said Nick. "I'm going to do some exploring." He set off for the dunes, whistling.

The dry sand in front of the dunes had been combed by the wind, and his footsteps were the first to disturb its crusted ripples. There were plenty of shells around. Broken clamshells crunched under his feet, and larger ones, some still hinged together, were scattered among the clumps of feathery grass.

A fishing lure, bright green against the gray sand, stared up at him with a round black eye. He picked it up and examined the rusted hook, thinking that Robbie might be able to use it. Beyond the next dune was a short length of rope and two pieces of silvered wood with rounded edges. More wood caught his eye—it looked like the corner of a box—and he stepped quickly over to it.

Something buried, that was for sure, with slats sticking up out of the sand. Using a large clamshell as a scoop, he dug at one side until he could get a foot under to pry it up. Then he pulled on the top until it came free.

Just an old crate; I might have known, he thought. But it had been almost covered over with sand. What a storm!

Farther on, he found chunks of Styrofoam caught in a tangle of dried seaweed and a half-buried coffee can. After a while, everything began to look the same—the hummocks of sand, the whispering grass, the shells.

He had just about decided that no pirate would bury treasure in a place like this when Robbie called to him from the beach. As he scuffed back through the sand, Nick talked to himself. "You've got to have a map or a cave or something. You can't expect to find it lying around out here."

"What're you muttering about?" Robbie asked. He frowned out at the ocean. "No, I didn't catch anything, so don't ask."

They trudged the rest of the way to the Inn without talking, and Nick thought ahead to the evening. Supper. Too bad Grandfather didn't eat with them. What had he done all day? Did he care that his grandsons were here at the Inn? Probably not.

While he changed clothes, Nick tried to remember what Mom had said about supper. Fried chicken? Right now, anything would taste good. Maybe there'd be party leftovers for dessert. Those strawberry tarts were fantastic, and so were the éclairs.

I wonder what kind of food Grandfather eats, he thought. Maybe he'd like an éclair.

He found his mother in the kitchen and told her his idea. "I was just fixing Grandfather's tray," she said. "I never know what to cook for him. He might enjoy something from the party."

She set a glass of milk on the tray. "Have you fed the cats yet?"

"Yes, this morning."

"I have to take some clean towels up to Grandfather," she said. "Would you like to carry the tray for me?"

"Sure."

Nick didn't know whether he was scared or just plain curious, but by the time they reached Grandfather's door, his hands were sweaty. He held tightly to the tray.

His mother knocked twice, then opened the door and stepped in. "Supper time!" she exclaimed, as though this were an exciting event. "Mrs. McHugh had her Tea this afternoon, and we brought you some party food. She's a wonderful cook!"

The room smelled stuffy; it was dark except for a pool of light around the bedside lamp. Nick's mother took the tray from him and bustled up to the bedside table, still chattering. "You should have seen the boys eat! Flora McHugh loved it—she likes to have her cooking appreciated that way. Here's Nicky. It was his idea to bring you one of the éclairs."

Nick stayed by the bureau, watching. The man looked lost in the big four-poster bed, a thin, shrunken figure propped up by pillows. One leg, enclosed in a cast, rested stiffly on top of the quilt. His face was half hidden by a faded red baseball cap, and he neither moved nor spoke. But Nick had the feeling of eyes upon him.

"Want me to help you sit up a little more?" Mom said cheerfully.

The old man grunted something. He raised a hand and waved her off.

"Okay then; I'll come up later to get the tray. Hope you enjoy your supper."

She turned so fast that Nick hardly had time to get out of her way. He looked back at the figure in the bed. "Good night, Grandfather," he said, in a voice that came out all scratchy. Then he hurried after his mother.

That evening Nick pulled out the papers his teacher had given him and tried to figure out what he should do for his study project. Some kind of living creature, like crabs, she'd said. Crabs? Hmm. He gazed at the cat on his bed. Cats? No, a cat would never do. Maybe he'd get an idea down at the beach. What was Robbie's project going to be?

"I don't know." Robbie looked blank when Nick asked about it. "Can't think of anything, but I guess I've got to get started—mine's a lot more complicated than yours."

"You could do fish," Nick said. "Since you like to go fishing all the time."

"That's a good idea. If I ever catch anything."

The next morning, Nick made sure he'd finished his chores by lunch time so he'd have plenty of time outside.

Today it seemed colder on the beach, and the wind had a cutting edge. At the foot of the steps, Robbie paused. "That hurricane sure messed up the fishing. I used to catch fish from the jetty all the time. Guess I'll try down here."

He turned left, away from the jetty, and Nick followed, picking up shells and tossing them into the waves as he went. When Robbie stopped to set up his pole, Nick hunched into his jacket and leaned back against the wind, looking around. The beach wasn't very wide here, and low sand dunes rose at its edge, with twiggy gray bushes and tall grasses growing behind them. Looked like he wasn't going to find any caves down this way either. The cold air numbed his fingers, and he curled his hands deep into his pockets.

He jiggled his feet to keep warm as he gazed down the empty beach. On the other side of the point, sea gulls were circling and dipping, rising and falling.

He called to Robbie against the wind. "I'm going to see what's over there."

His brother waved, and Nick strolled close to the water, scattering the tiny birds that dashed in and out of the waves. Just around the point, he stopped. A tall man stood in the surf with sea gulls whirling around his head. On the wind came their mewling cries and fragments of the words he called to them.

Nick headed up toward the dunes, trying to look purposeful, glancing back as he went. The man wore waders like Robbie's, and a heavy green jacket, but no cap on his short black hair. He was throwing something to the gulls—maybe bread? One or two birds had landed on his shoulders, but most of them snatched at the food as they swooped past.

Fast food, thought Nick, and grinned to himself. He slowed his pace to watch.

The man tossed the last few pieces high in the air, and the gulls dipped low, skimming the water to catch each one. As he turned, his voice came clearly on the wind. "That's all for now, my beauties. See you tomorrow." He splashed back onto the beach and crossed the sand with long strides. He was heading for the dunes behind Nick.

Nick wanted to disappear into the bushes, but it was too late.

"Hi there," the man said. "Nice day for flying, isn't it?"

Nick only nodded, not sure what he meant.

The man paused, gazing back at the ocean. His face was dark brown, lined with wrinkles. "Ever wish you were a gull?" he asked. "You could take the wings of the morning and fly to an island, far out at sea—" He stopped and grinned down at Nick. "Actually, these birds do have islands where they go every year to raise their young." He gave Nick a friendly wave and walked farther into the dunes.

Must be a path back in there, Nick thought. Might be worth exploring. He watched until the man's head disappeared behind a clump of bushes.

When they got back to the Inn, Nick told his mother about the man and the gulls. He wiggled his fingers in the warmth of the kitchen. "I wonder what he was feeding them."

"That's nice," his mother said. She stood still, staring out the kitchen window. Usually she was bouncing around the kitchen, her dark hair swinging and her hands flying from one project to the next.

"How's Grandfather doing?" he asked.

She squinted her eyes like she did when she had a headache. "One of the cats got into his room, and he threw a half-empty soda can at it. What a mess!"

"Where's the cat now?"

"Nobody knows. It might still be in there."

"I'll call them for supper," said Nick, "then we can tell."

But only the two big black cats came to eat. The striped gray one was missing, and he'd already checked his bedroom.

His mother sighed. "You'll have to go into your grandfather's room and get it," she said. "Or he'll keep us up all night."

"How about if we propped the door open. Don't you think—"

She shook her head. "He'd hate that. Please, Nicky."

4
That Wretched Feline

Nick stood outside Grandfather's room for a minute, trying to remember how the furniture was arranged. Maybe the old man would be taking a nap.

I'll grab the cat and be out in a minute, he thought.

Silently he turned the doorknob, then he slipped into the dark room. Raspy breathing came from the bed.

He dropped to his knees. The cat was probably under something. He crawled over to the bureau and swished a hand through the shadows. Not there. He lay flat to peer under the bed. Nothing. I should have brought a flashlight, he thought. He sat up and looked around, unwilling to go closer to the sleeping man. What about behind those long drapes?

Slowly, cautiously, he crawled across the room. He slid behind the drapes, then looked up at the dim outline of a window seat. As he pulled himself up onto the cushions, a furry shadow stirred. He put a hand on the cat's back.

Leaning close to the window, he gazed out at the dusky sky. Past the top of a pine tree lay sand dunes and a wilderness of bushes. A pair of gulls glimmered in the twilight as they flew back and forth.

This window faces the same direction as mine, he thought, stroking the cat. She purred loudly under his hand.

"What? What?" growled a voice. "Is that wretched feline back in here?" The lamp clicked on.

Nick took a deep breath and spoke up, trying to sound businesslike. "Sorry, I was just taking her out." As he picked up the cat, she dug her claws into the cushions of the window seat. He yanked hard, then stumbled backwards through the drapes. He had to stop and adjust his hold on the squirming cat.

The man in the bed was glaring at him, and the veins on his skinny neck bulged out alarmingly. Was he going to have a heart attack?

Nick tried to think of something to calm the old man down. The baseball cap? He couldn't see the emblem on it. "Are you a Phillies fan, Grandfather?"

"Nope." A thin hand reached up to settle the cap more firmly in place. "It's the Cardinals for me—always will be—"

"Nicky!" His mother stood in the hall, whispering frantically. "Come here with that cat!"

He left, wondering what Grandfather had been about to say.

Later on, when they were doing the dishes together, Nick told Robbie what had happened and how the old man wore a baseball cap in bed.

His brother's face darkened. "Why does he have to be such a grouch? Don't be afraid of him."

"I'm not afraid of him."

Robbie smiled in that superior way of his. "You sure?"

"Sure."

"Prove it."

Nick picked up a handful of forks and almost dropped them. "What do you mean?"

"Go in there sometime and look at him when he's sleeping." Robbie flicked a cluster of soap bubbles high into the air. "I want to know if he sleeps in that baseball cap all night."

Nick tried to sound bored. "Well, I might, some time." He turned and clattered the forks into the drawer.

For the rest of the evening, Nick's thoughts circled around his grandfather. Of course he wasn't afraid of him. The old man was just . . . *ornery*. But for now, he'd stay out of Grandfather's way.

He tried to think about something else. Tomorrow he could explore the beach some more and maybe get an idea for his school project.

The next afternoon as they walked down the beach, Nick asked Robbie about the man who fed the gulls.

"Who? Oh, the Japanese guy. I think Mom got to know him last year. She said he's a Christian."

Ahead of them, sea gulls swirled against the blue sky. "I'm going to see what's on the other side of the point," said Nick.

"Me too. I think I'll try over there today."

They rounded the point, and when Robbie turned down toward the water, Nick kept to the high tide line, near the dunes.

He scanned the beach, looking for the gull man.

There. The man stood farther down the shore, surrounded by gulls. He waved when Robbie stopped to set up his pole. Nick collected a handful of shells, then he sauntered down to the water, taking a roundabout path. The gulls paid no attention to him. They screamed and called to each other, dipping and rising on powerful wings, snatching at whatever the man threw to them.

"Hello," said the man. "Are you visiting at the Inn?"

"Well, sort of," Nick said. "My mom's taking care of it for a couple of weeks."

"Oh, yes, Mrs. Radford. I've met her." He inclined his head, and for a minute Nick thought he was going to bow. "I am Takashi Yoshimura. My friends call me Kashi." He pronounced his name with a soft *a*, like the *a* in *wash*. Smiling, he waved a hand at the gulls. "These rascals don't bother with names. They just go for the food."

"I was wondering what you feed them," said Nick.

"Raisin bread," said Kashi. "The iron in the raisins is good for them—makes them strong."

"They sure look strong," said Nick. "Like that one." He squinted at a gull soaring high above the others.

Kashi watched it too. "They've got streamlined bodies and hollow bones. And God gave them wings that are long and flexible, tapered just right. That's why they can fly so high."

They stood in companionable silence until Nick felt the cold creeping under his jacket and decided to move around. He trotted farther down the beach, tossing his shells into the water, one by one. The same little birds he'd seen yesterday skittered back and forth in front of him, as though they were playing tag with the waves.

What kind of birds are they, he wondered, remembering his study project. Kashi would probably know. He jogged for a while, then turned back, eyeing the birds with new interest.

Kashi looked as though he were about to leave, so Nick hurried over to him. "Sure are a lot of birds around here," he said. "What kind are they?"

"The little ones with skinny legs are sanderlings," Kashi said. "Most of the others are herring gulls—they've got gray backs and white heads. The ones with black heads are called laughing gulls. That's because their cry sounds like a crazy sort of *ha-ha-ha*."

Nick ignored Robbie, who was waving at him. "What's that big gull over there?" he asked.

"That's a great black-backed gull." Kashi threw out one last piece of bread and crumpled up his plastic bag. "I know your name too. You must be the Nicky that this big guy has been calling."

He grinned at Robbie, who was clumping over the sand toward them. "Looks like your brother is ready to go home." Kashi lifted his face to the breeze that blew from the ocean. "We might be getting some bad weather. But maybe I'll see you tomorrow."

On their way back to the Inn, Nick tried naming the different kinds of gulls. "I think I'll do my study project on birds," he told Robbie. "Maybe just sea gulls. Kashi told me some stuff about them."

"Who's Kashi? Oh, him." Robbie kicked up little puffs of sand as he walked. "I thought maybe I'd do fish like you said, but not if I never catch any. It was high tide today too." He was silent for a minute, then he grinned. "Or I could write a manual on fifty ways not to catch a fish. With diagrams."

The aroma of something chocolate met them as they stepped through the kitchen door. "Smells wonderful," Nick said to his mother. "What is it?"

"Chocolate fudge cake," she said. "I found out that it's Archie's favorite, and I wanted to cheer him up. But now there's a pile of dishes for you, and I'm going to be late with supper. It's about time you two were back."

Nick got started on the dishes right away. "What's the matter with Archie?"

"Something about the book he's writing." Nick's mother took a bag of carrots out of the refrigerator. "He'll be glad to tell you all about it, I'm sure. But not now. I'm so late! Maybe you'd better leave those dishes and peel some carrots for me. Rob, could you start on a salad?"

A buzzer sounded, somewhere at the other end of the kitchen. "Oh, no! That's your grandfather. He's probably wondering where his supper is. He likes it early."

She cut up a tomato and added it to a plate of food on the counter. "Okay, he's got his chicken and some peas. Maybe some Jell-O for dessert. And here's a glass of milk. I'm not giving him another can of soda."

She sent Nick a worried glance. "Would you mind taking the tray up to him?"

"Okay." He knew she'd probably been up the stairs a dozen times already, answering Grandfather's buzzer.

At Grandfather's door he knocked twice, just as his mother had, then he went in, wishing he could think of something cheerful to say. Grandfather was sitting up, still wearing the red baseball cap. He wore earphones too; they were plugged into a small TV set. He glanced up from the soccer game on the screen, looking impatient.

"I brought your supper," Nick said. "Mom's running late tonight."

The old man grunted a reply and pulled off his earphones. Nick concentrated on getting the tray onto the bedside table without spilling anything.

"What's so great about the Phillies?" Grandfather asked abruptly. "They've only made it to the World Series four times. But the *Cards*—well, back in the '64 Series, the Cards beat Mickey Mantle and the Yankees—even though Mantle got three homers. The Phillies never did anything like that, did they?" Without waiting for an answer, he asked, "Play baseball, boy?"

"A little," Nick said. Then he had to add, "I'm not very good at it."

"Ever see any games—real ones—close up?"

"We went to Philadelphia a couple of times—"

"Phillies!" The old man spit out the name, as if he'd tasted something bad. "Well, I guess you can't help it."

Nick shifted uncomfortably. "Do you want anything else for supper?" He eyed Mom's carefully arranged plate. It didn't look like very much.

"Junk food, boy, that's what I crave. Hot dogs. French fries. Pizza."

He picked up his fork and stabbed at the Jell-O. "Look at all this healthy stuff."

"Maybe you need good food for your leg—"

"Don't tell me what I need for my leg. You're as bad as all these women swarming around, telling me what to do. It's enough to drive a man wild."

Nick started backing up. "Okay." What was it Mom had said? "We'll stop by later for your dishes."

He made it out of the room before his grandfather could say anything else, and closed the door quickly. Then he had to grin to himself. Junk food, huh? And still wearing that baseball cap. The old guy couldn't be all bad.

After supper that night, Nick went out onto the veranda to see whether a storm was coming, as Kashi had said. Sure enough, there was no moon, and clouds had swallowed up the stars. Leaning on the rail, he listened to the swish of waves on the beach below. He pictured them rushing in, dark as night, tipped with white foam. At the far end of the veranda, a shadowy figure rose. Nick jerked to attention, but it was only Archie, getting up from a chair. The red-haired man paced up and down, muttering to himself; finally he stopped beside Nick.

"How're you doing, Nicky? Your mom sure makes a great fudge cake, doesn't she?"

"She sure does."

Archie gazed out at the ocean. " 'Twas a dark and stormy night . . ." He sounded as though he were quoting something, and his deep voice made it spooky. " 'Twas on a night such as this, the Flageltines first descended to earth. Some rode on stormy clouds, and others slid down on bolts of lightning. Crashing thunder hid the sound of their war cries."

Nick glanced up at him in amazement. What was he talking about?

Archie chuckled. "Well, how does it sound so far?"

"Uh, sort of weird," Nick said. "Is that from a book you're reading?"

"Nope. It's a book I'm writing." Archie sounded pleased, and Nick decided that he'd said the right thing.

A moment later, Archie said, "Well, I thought I was writing it. I even brought my dad's old typewriter to use—for inspiration—you know? But now I'm stuck. And I've only got until Christmas." He sighed. "Now, here's the basic plot—"

He explained about the Flageltines, why they were fighting with the earthlings. Something about an ancient Scots chieftain who had betrayed his clan. Nick couldn't make much sense of it, and the more Archie explained, the more he began to wonder whether he should be working on his school project.

Archie stopped for breath. "So, what do you think? Maybe I should start over again. Hmmm. It wasn't perfectly clear to you, was it? A plot outline—that might help. Thanks a lot, Nicky!"

He disappeared inside, and a minute later Nick followed him. He really did need to get started on his study notebook. First, he'd write down what Kashi had told him about the different kinds of gulls.

Nick woke that night to the sound of rain drumming on his window. By midmorning the rain had stopped, but dark clouds hung low over the water, and the wind blew in sharp gusts. He hurried to finish his chores, wondering whether Robbie would still go fishing.

Robbie shrugged. "I don't care—the rain's not going to stop me," his brother said. "You coming?"

"Keep an eye on the weather, boys," called Mom as they left. "And don't stay out if it begins to storm."

5

Bubbles in the Think Tank

Kashi was there, just as Nick had hoped. Today the gulls looked like snowflakes swirling out of the dull sky. He raced across the sand toward them.

"Hi there," said Kashi. "So you're not just a fair-weather friend?"

Nick shrugged, like Robbie had. "Rain doesn't bother me." He raised his voice against the wind and the gulls' cries. "What about them?"

Kashi waved at the circling birds. "Doesn't bother them either. Their feathers keep them warm and dry. And they love the wind."

Far above them a gull sailed higher and higher. "How can it do that without flapping its wings?" asked Nick.

"It catches a wind current or an updraft—and hitchhikes a ride." Kashi's eyes gleamed. They were dark brown, full of light and warmth. "You sure ask a lot of questions. You writing a book?"

"It's a project for school," said Nick. "I might do sea gulls."

"They're fascinating," Kashi agreed. "I like to watch them fly—that's why I feed them."

The wind flung sand against Nick's legs and sent icy drafts down his neck. He pulled his hood more tightly about his head, then ran down the beach until he was out of breath.

Finally he turned and walked back, watching how the gulls held their wings as they flew.

"Getting plenty cold, isn't it?" Kashi asked. "How about you and your brother coming to my place for some hot chocolate?"

"Sure!"

When he asked Robbie, his brother said, "Okay. I was just thinking I'd had enough for today."

They followed Kashi into the wilderness behind the dunes. The bushes were tall enough to shield them from the wind, and they made Nick feel as though he were walking through a miniature forest, gray-barked and leafless. On some of the bushes grew round gray berries.

"What kind of bushes are these?" he asked.

"Bayberry," said Robbie. He scraped off a cluster of the waxy fruits and tossed them to his brother. "Don't eat 'em—but birds think they're good. I read somewhere that people used to make candles from them too."

Kashi's house was a long white cottage tucked into a clump of pine trees. On its roof stood a bronze weathervane shaped like a large gull. That looks like a great black-backed gull, Nick thought, proud to have remembered the name.

"Take off your coats—sit down, sit down." Kashi bustled about in his small kitchen, putting a kettle of water on the stove, setting out spoons and tall red mugs.

Soon he was pouring cocoa into their mugs. "Let's sit in here." He led the way into the living room where cushioned chairs were arranged in front of a fireplace. The fragrance of chocolate and cinnamon rose from Nick's cup as he eased into a chair; he took a careful sip. Hot, but good.

Robbie nudged him, almost spilling his cocoa. "Look over there." At the far end of the room, a huge Oriental face glared down from the wall. Beside it clung a giant-sized insect with round yellow eyes and a long body that was striped red, yellow, and green.

Nick took a closer look. "Kites!" he exclaimed. The wall was covered with kites of different sizes and colors. One, shaped like a red star, had long red and white streamers that reached all the way to the floor.

"You boys fly kites?" asked Kashi, setting down his mug.

Nick shook his head.

Robbie's eyes were still on the kites. "I used to, but I've never seen any like yours."

"Ever make your own?"

"You made these?" asked Robbie.

"Sure did." Kashi lifted down the angry face. "This is a warrior kite, a hero from the ancient Japanese stories. He's getting old, so I don't fly him anymore."

Nick studied a kite shaped like a brown bird; it seemed to have real feathers on its wings. "Are they hard to make?"

"Not really, once you know how."

While Robbie and Kashi talked, Nick gazed at the wall of kites and slowly drank his cocoa.

Before long, rain pattered at the window, and it was time to go. Kashi waved good-bye as they started down the sandy path, and Nick turned for a last look at the sea gull weathervane.

That evening he wrote in his diary for school about Kashi's weathervane and the wall of kites. The red star was his favorite. He could just see those streamers fluttering in the wind. When he worked on his sea gull notebook, he added what Kashi had said about the birds riding on wind currents, but he put a question mark in the margin. He'd have to find out some more from Kashi.

That night, kites and sea gulls mingled in his dreams. One especially large black-backed gull flew down and settled onto the weathervane on Kashi's house.

He awoke early, still thinking about the weathervane, wondering whether he could see it from here. He got to his knees and looked out past the pine tree. No, he wasn't high enough. How about Grandfather's window? When he'd taken the cat off the window seat, he'd seen the top of a pine tree. It was probably this same tree.

Nick propped his elbows on the sill, wondering what everything would look like from the highest window in the house. He'd be able to see the weathervane from up there. Besides, the old man would be asleep. He could check on that baseball cap.

Did he dare try it? Why not? Grandfather hadn't noticed him last time, not until the cat had started purring.

Nick dressed quickly, leaving off his sneakers, then he climbed the stairway without making a sound and tiptoed down the hall. The doorknob turned silently in his hand, as before. He crept inside and pushed the door almost shut.

Darkness lay like a curtain in front of him, but he knew the window was straight ahead. Just in case Grandfather had one eye open, he stayed low, feeling his way along the floor. Maybe he'd find out about the cap some other day.

The bed sheets rustled, and he froze. He waited for a long time before sliding one foot forward again.

The drapes parted easily as he pulled himself up toward the gray rectangle of the window. He knelt to look out.

Mist lay over the bushes like smoke, but he soon figured out where Kashi's house would be. As he waited, sea gulls winged past in the brightening sky. Slowly the mist parted; he leaned forward. Yes, there was a low gray roof; at one end, something moved, glinting in the sun. Nick smiled to himself.

"Who's that?" Grandfather's hoarse whisper cut the air. "Come out of there, you."

Nick gripped the sill.

"Come on—I've been listening to you."

He stumbled through the drapes, finding it hard to breathe, and wishing he at least had the cat for an excuse.

The lamp clicked on. Grandfather pulled himself upright with surprising speed and clapped the baseball cap onto his head. He waved a skinny arm at Nick. "Come closer, boy."

Nick took two reluctant steps forward, and the small, wrinkled face stared up at him. "So what are you doing in my room?"

Nick swallowed. He searched for some words.

"Well? Cat got your tongue? Heh. Heh. Heh."

Was that a cough, or was the old man laughing at him?

"Not after a cat this time, were you? So what made you come back?"

"The window. I wanted to see . . ." Nick backed toward the door.

"And you thought the old coot would never notice? What's so interesting outside that window of mine?"

"Well, there's this man who lives out there—" Nick gestured wildly. "And he feeds the sea gulls, and he talked to me about them, and he has this weathervane on his roof, so I—"

"He *feeds* the sea gulls? Is he three bricks short of a load?"

Nick stared. "What's that?"

"You know—bubbles in the think tank. Nobody home upstairs. *Who* in his right mind would feed sea gulls?"

"There's nothing wrong with Kashi's mind." Nick's voice rose. "He's teaching me all kinds of stuff about gulls. And you should see the kites he makes—he's really smart . . ."

The old man's eyes burned into him, but Nick didn't care, not after what he'd said about Kashi. "I'm sorry—I'll leave right away."

He closed the door quietly and ran downstairs to his room. "Bubbles in the think tank!" Grandfather just didn't know Kashi.

Slowly Nick put on his sneakers. He hadn't had much time to look at the weathervane, but at least he'd found out about the baseball cap.

Robbie hadn't asked lately whether he'd tried to catch Grandfather asleep. Maybe his brother would ask again this morning.

Finally, that afternoon on their way down the beach, Nick said, "Well, I found out." He gathered a handful of shells and rattled them happily.

"What?"

"About the baseball cap. He doesn't wear it to sleep in."

"Oh." Robbie sounded disappointed. "How do you know?"

"I went in there this morning, real early."

Robbie shot him a suspicious glance. "You just walked right in?"

"Well, I sort of crept in. I wanted to see if I could find Kashi's weathervane from that window of his." Nick tossed a shell into the air and caught it.

"And he was asleep?"

"Guess so. He heard me and sat up and put on the cap real fast."

"What'd he say?"

After Nick told him, Robbie made a face and stared down the beach. "He's always been a grouchy old buzzard. And he hates kids. He ought to be doing something useful instead of hassling you. He should be up out of bed, exercising that leg like Alex used to. Remember when Alex broke his leg? Grandfather just wants Mom to wait on him."

He glanced sideways at Nick. "How come you're all the time worrying about him?"

At least Robbie hadn't said anything about being afraid. "I don't know," Nick said. "Sometimes I don't even like him very much."

A herring gull swooped past them with a clam in its beak. They stopped to watch as it rose high in the air and let the clam drop. "He ought to try that over a parking lot," Robbie said. "It'd crack open a lot easier."

"Who?" Nick asked, still thinking about Grandfather.

"That sea gull. Hey!" Robbie waved toward the point ahead. "Your friend's got one of his kites up. Why don't you ask if he'll show us how to make 'em?"

"Okay." Nick ran across the sand with renewed energy. The kite was round and white, with a hole in the center and huge black-and-white eyes. It soared above the water, looking like a strange white bird itself.

He slowed as he reached Kashi, looking to see whether the hovering gulls noticed the kite. It didn't seem to bother them, although a brownish-colored gull on Kashi's shoulder kept trying to peck at the kite string.

"What's your kite supposed to be?" asked Nick.

Kashi glanced up at the kite. "It's a fish they have in Japan, called a blowfish."

"What's that hole in the center? Its mouth?"

"Right." Kashi handed the kite string to Nick. "Here, you want to try it? Just keep the line taut and don't let go."

"Okay." Nick stood still, the kite tugging at the string in his hand as though it had a life of its own. He had to tip his head way back to watch it. Seemed to be doing fine.

"Do you think you'd ever have time to show us how to build some kites?"

"I think so," Kashi said. "Let's see. I'm not working Saturday afternoon. Bring some big pieces of cloth or plastic. I've got enough wood and string."

"Great!" Nick exclaimed. "I'm sure we can find some stuff."

When Kashi had finished feeding the gulls, most of them flew off, but the brownish one stayed on his shoulder. "What kind is he?" asked Nick, wishing he had a cracker in his pocket. "I like his brown spots."

"He's a teenaged laughing gull," Kashi said. "When he molts, he'll lose those brown spots; then he'll look just like his parents and grandparents."

Grandparents. That made Nick think about Grandfather. Would he look like Grandfather when he was old? Would he act like him?

"Let's take the kite down and go for a walk," said Kashi. "I always like to check out the dunes after a storm." He reached for the kite string, and the brown gull flew off. "You got something on your mind?"

"Well, sort of." Nick kept his eyes on the gull in the sky. "I've got this grandfather, see, and he's . . . well, Robbie calls him an old buzzard—tough and grouchy."

"Where does he live?"

"He's staying at the Inn. Aunt Margo has to take care of him because he broke his leg. He used to live by himself up in New York, but we didn't visit him much. After my dad died, we never went at all. Now Mom's taking care of the Inn, and he's about as ornery as he can be."

Nick stopped to pick up a round white stone. Its rough edges had been worn smooth by the waves, and he liked the feel of it.

"So now you're getting to know him?"

"A little," Nick said. "He likes baseball—wears a Cardinals hat, even in bed. I talked to him a couple of times, but he just gets mad at me." He tossed the stone up in the air and caught it. "Guess I sort of deserved it this morning."

"I've known people like that." Kashi looked thoughtful. "Perhaps he has nothing to live for."

Nick considered. "He doesn't know God."

"That would make a difference. Does he get around much?"

"No, he just stays in bed all the time. We knew a kid who broke his leg, and the doctor made him get up to exercise it. Robbie says Grandfather won't even try because he wants Mom to wait on him."

"What does your mother say?"

Nick scuffed at a clump of seaweed. "She says to pray."

Kashi nodded. "Good for her. God is the only one who can change a heart. I've learned that."

Nick didn't say anything. Mom seemed to be hoping for some kind of miracle. Sure, he wouldn't mind having a real grandfather. He'd even started praying for Grandfather. But so far, it didn't seem like God was doing very much.

Kashi put a hand on his shoulder, and Nick looked up into the lined brown face. "Don't give up on your grandfather, Nick."

A big black dog trotted slowly past them, holding its tail high. "There's Chaucer," said Kashi. "Flora McHugh must be out looking for driftwood."

Nick didn't mind changing the subject. "What does she do with all those pieces of wood?"

"She and Tina decorate them with shells, then they sell them to a gift shop."

"Tina?"

"That's her daughter. She comes up on the weekends sometimes. You probably haven't met her yet." Kashi chuckled. "You'd remember Tina."

"Good afternoon, Mr. Yoshimura." Mrs. McHugh stood in the dunes, demolishing a heap of seaweed with her stick. "We missed you on Sunday."

"Hello, Mrs. McHugh." Kashi inclined his head politely. "I would have come to your tea party, but they called me in for an ambulance flight."

She smiled at him, her angular face softening. "Then I'll look forward to seeing you this week. Tina will be here too." She picked up a battered piece of wood, waved it triumphantly, and marched farther into the dunes.

She had paid no attention to Nick, and it didn't bother him at all. "Are you a pilot?" he asked Kashi.

"Yes. Supposed to be retired, but they need me every once in a while." He glanced at his watch. "That reminds me. I have a flight this evening. It's almost 4:00, and I'd better get back."

"Me too!" exclaimed Nick. "Robbie's probably ready to go. See you." He turned and raced down the beach.

Robbie was waiting. He'd even stowed all his fishing gear. "Did you ask him about making kites?"

"Yep. He said Saturday. All we have to do is bring some cloth or plastic."

Later, while Nick was peeling potatoes for supper, his mother said quietly, "Your grandfather asked for you to come up and see him."

"What's the matter?"

"I don't know." But she looked unhappy.

With the tip of his knife, Nick dug at an eye in the potato. "I'm sorry," he said. "I keep getting in trouble with him. I just wanted—"

"It's not your fault, Nicky. I know you mean well." The buzzer sounded from the other end of the kitchen, insistent and shrill, as though Grandfather himself were complaining to them.

His mother swung toward the stove. "Oh, that's right. He wants you to bring his supper tray up to him too. I'll have it ready in a minute."

"Sure." He finished up the potatoes and thought about what Kashi had said. He wouldn't give up on Grandfather . . . not yet.

6
Junk Food

He checked the food on the tray after his mother had arranged it. Chicken casserole that smelled good. Green beans. Salad. Fruit in a dessert dish. Not exactly junk food. Was there any of Archie's fudge cake left? Yes. While he was cutting a slice, his mother said, "Not before supper, Nicky. Besides, I was saving that cake—"

"It's for Grandfather. I think he needs it." She gave him a puzzled glance but didn't say anything more, and he hurried upstairs with the tray. Grandfather was sitting up, waiting.

"Right down here, boy."

Nick set the tray carefully on the blanket in front of the old man.

"What's this? Cake?" Grandfather poked at the fudge cake with one bony finger.

Nick watched him. "It's the closest I could get to junk food."

"Yes siree!" Grandfather touched the brim of his cap as if he were saluting, then he picked up the cake and took a big bite. He hadn't even tasted anything else. Good thing Mom isn't here, Nick thought.

Grandfather took another bite, and then he said, "Home-made, huh?"

"Yes, Mom made it for Archie because it's his favorite and he needed cheering up."

"Who is Archie, and why does he need cheering up?" Grandfather licked the frosting off his fingers.

Nick leaned against a bedpost."Well, he's a guy who's staying here. He's writing a book, and I don't think it was going very well. I heard his typewriter this morning. Maybe he's doing better."

"Hmm." Grandfather finished the cake and started on the rest of his meal. "So did you see any more of that amazing person who feeds gulls? What's his name?"

"Takashi Yoshimura." Nick pronounced it with dignity, as Kashi had.

"Japanese, huh?" said Grandfather. "I might have known."

Something about the old man's comment annoyed Nick, but he kept talking. "He said to call him Kashi. He showed me a teenaged gull. It's got brownish spots right now, but after it molts, it'll look like those black-headed laughing gulls." He grinned, remembering. "It sat on his shoulder and kept pecking at the kite string."

"Flying kites, was he?"

"Yes, at first I thought his kite was some kind of bird—"

"—Nicky? Are you going to eat supper?" That was Robbie, calling up the stairs.

"Guess they're waiting for me." He turned toward the door, then paused, adding shyly, "Maybe I'll see you tomorrow."

Grandfather waved a fork at him. "How about bringing up my breakfast?"

After supper, Nick reminded Robbie about getting some cloth for their kites.

"That's right; we'd better check it out. Mom thinks there are some old sheets in the attic."

It didn't take long to get the sheets, but the attic wasn't nearly as mysterious as Nick had hoped. No old trunks or boxes from India or secret diaries. Not at all like the attics the Hemming Brothers explored.

The next morning, first thing, Nick remembered what Grandfather had said about bringing breakfast up to him. His mother smiled when he told her. "That would be a help. Do you mind?"

"No. Sometimes he's not so bad."

Outside the bedroom door, he paused before knocking. "Please, Lord, help me to know what to say to him," he prayed silently. Maybe this would be one of Grandfather's better days.

"Come in."

The bedside light was on, and he wore the baseball cap at a jaunty angle. Was that a good sign? But he scowled as Nick stepped through the doorway. "What in tarnation was all that noise in the hall last night?"

"We went into the attic to get some sheets, and we had to pull down the folding stairs to get there." Nick delivered the tray and edged closer to the door in case he said to get out.

"Sheets? Come over here, boy. I don't bite." He glanced down at his tray. "Pancakes! That's a big improvement. How'd you manage that?"

"Mom made them for us," Nick said. "Thought you might want some."

"Well, we seem to think alike on the matter of food." Grandfather poured a cascade of syrup over the pancakes and licked his lips.

"Okay now." He paused to eat a dripping forkful. "Sit down and tell me about the sheets. What're they for?"

Nick perched on the edge of the bed. "For kites. Tomorrow Kashi is going to help me and Robbie make our own."

"You said something before about this man's kites. He has a lot of them?"

"Yes, a bunch. We saw them at his house—a whole wall of kites. There's one that looks like a star—a red star with streamers. Yesterday he was flying a blowfish kite. It's Japanese. Have you ever seen one?"

"A blowfish or a Japanese?"

"Well, a blowfish," said Nick. "It's big and round with a huge mouth in the center and—"

"I know, I know."

"He told me that the people in Japan really like blowfish. I wonder how come—"

"They call it *fugu*," interrupted Grandfather. "It's considered a delicacy; I've got to admit it tastes pretty good."

Nick looked at him curiously. "Sounds like you've been to Japan."

"Yes, I have," said Grandfather. "Unfortunately." He frowned at his coffee cup. "This stuff is cold."

"It's a cold day," said Nick. "Want me to get you some in a Thermos?"

Grandfather looked surprised, then he shrugged. "It's worth a try."

By the time Nick got back with his coffee, Grandfather had finished eating. His plate looked remarkably clean, and Nick wondered whether he'd licked the syrup off it.

Walking past the window gave him an idea. "If I open the drapes, you can look outside," he said. "It's a nice day out there."

Grandfather didn't object. As Nick pulled the drapes open, a large gull sailed by. "That's a great black-backed gull," Nick remarked. "Kashi says they fly like an eagle—they're so majestic."

He glanced at his grandfather, who seemed to be watching him instead of looking out the window. "Can you see out from your bed?"

"A little. I got a glimpse of that great black-backed gull," said Grandfather. "How come you're so interested in gulls, anyway?"

"Kashi got me started. I'm going to use gulls for my school project." Nick took another look out the window. "No kites out there today. Kashi had to work."

Grandfather put down his coffee cup and leaned back against the pillows. "Where'd he get all those kites?"

"He made some of them," Nick said. "I'll ask him about the others." He wished it were Saturday already.

Late Friday night, Mrs. McHugh's daughter arrived, and by Saturday morning everyone in the Inn knew Tina was there. She didn't actually shout, but her voice was shrill, and she spoke with a great deal of energy.

Even Grandfather asked about her over his breakfast tray. "Who belongs to that piercing female voice I heard this morning?"

"That's Tina." Nick grinned. "Mrs. McHugh's daughter, but you'd never know it. She has lots of blond hair—the curly kind—and big blue eyes. Sort of pretty, I guess."

"Is she plump?"

"Yes, but she sure gets around fast. She asked Mom if they could use the dining room to work on those driftwood things they make, and a few minutes later she had stuff all over the place."

"Stuff?"

"Dried flowers and pieces of fur and feathers and little shells. And chunks of driftwood."

Grandfather grunted. "One of those crafty types. They scare me to death." Then he grinned.

Maybe Grandfather was improving just a bit, Nick thought. As he carried the tray downstairs, he prayed for him again.

When Nick checked his list, he saw that he was supposed to vacuum the dining room that morning, but the women were working there, and Chaucer lay under one of the tables. He decided to wait until the project was over. For now, he'd dust the antiques on the back shelves. Tina was having a spirited discussion with her mother about whether she should add lace edging to one particular lampshade, and Mrs. McHugh was gluing eyes onto a pair of driftwood dogs.

Nick was dusting some tattered cookbooks when Mrs. McHugh glanced up and saw him. "Landsakes!" She raised her voice. "What are you doing there, lad?" Before he could answer, she spoke to her daughter. "Kind of sneaky, don't you think, that boy standing back there, listening to us?"

"No, Mama, he's just doing his work," said Tina absent-mindedly.

"Humph. My Malcolm always used to say, 'Never trust a quiet boy.' Now what do you think about black tails on these dogs?"

Nick decided he'd shake out the cloth and finish dusting another time. He was cleaning the big mirror in the hall when Mrs. McHugh came past.

"My daughter said you were dusting, lad. I didn't mean for you to leave your work. Do you like our driftwood creations? That's what Tina calls them. "

She handed him a driftwood dog. While he examined it, she said, "I hear that Mr. Yoshimura is going to help you lads build some kites today. I'm glad he's taken an interest in you. A fine man he is; a fine man indeed."

After she left, Nick wondered how she knew about the kites. Kashi must have told her. They seemed to be old friends.

That afternoon at Kashi's house, Nick remembered Grandfather's curiosity about the wall of kites. Perhaps he could find out something today.

There wasn't time to ask, not at first. Kashi said they would make simple kites to begin with, and he gave them the bamboo sticks he liked to use. After they had notched the sticks and tied them together, Kashi showed them how to bend the crosswise stick and tie it securely.

"This is the bow stick," he said. "It helps make the kite stable and easier to fly." His nimble brown hands worked quickly with the kite string.

"No tail, huh?" asked Robbie.

Kashi smiled. "That's right. My grandfather always said that a well-built kite doesn't need a tail—it'll fly better and need less wind without one. Other things can help a kite fly. See how the warrior kite has those yellow tassels on the sides?"

"Yes." Robbie went over to the wall for a closer look.

"A good kite flier knows how to adjust them. Sometimes he'll trim them to make his kite fly better."

Kashi tossed a ball of string to Robbie. "We'll outline the frame with string, then cut out the covering." After they had done that, he asked, "Do you boys want to decorate your kites? Now's the time—before we glue on the covering. I've got some spray paint you can use."

"Red," said Nick hopefully. "I'd like red spots."

Robbie's cloth was striped yellow. "Maybe yellow trim for mine," he said.

While they were waiting for the paint to dry, Nick remembered to ask Kashi about his collection. "How'd you get interested in kites?"

"My grandfather was a professional kite maker in Japan," said Kashi. "He had to work in a store when he came to this country, but he still made kites in his spare time. I liked to watch him."

"Grandfather looked interested when I told him about your kites," said Nick. That gave him an idea. "As long as you're coming to Mrs. McHugh's Tea on Sunday, I could take you up to meet him."

"We could do that." Kashi's expression was grave. "Are you sure he won't mind?"

Nick remembered the undercurrent of dislike in his Grandfather's voice when he spoke of Kashi. "It's hard to tell," he said, uneasy now. He bent over his kite and smoothed down the edges, taking more time than was necessary. He hoped desperately that Grandfather wouldn't mind.

Nick had wanted to fly their kites right away, but when they finished, it was late, and Kashi said it was too windy. They bundled up their kites and hurried through the wind-tossed bushes. Nick clutched at his kite, thinking that Kashi had been right about the wind; it was getting dark too. Mom would be starting supper and waiting for them to help her. He wondered whether Mrs. McHugh and Tina had left their stuff spread all over the dining room.

Except for two empty tables, the dining room still looked like a craft shop, but neither of the women worked there that evening. Nick was wondering why when his mother reminded him about tomorrow's Tea. "Let's get the kitchen cleaned up fast," she said. "Tina and her mother want to get started on their baking."

"Oh, I forgot to tell you," said Nick. "Since Kashi's coming for the Tea, I asked him if he'd come up and talk to Grandfather."

Nick's mother gave him a worried glance. "What's he going to talk to your Grandfather about?"

"Well, they both like kites, I think. And what I'm really hoping is that Kashi will say something to Grandfather about God. You told me how God needs to change Grandfather's heart. And I've been praying for him. Maybe this is how God's going to do it."

"Maybe," his mother said. "If your grandfather will listen. Better ask him if it's all right for Mr. Yoshimura to visit."

7
It's a Kite-Eating Bush

When Nick delivered Grandfather's tray the next morning, he started telling him about the Tea right away.

"They made a big cheesecake. And I heard Tina say something this morning about frosted strawberries."

"Not bad," Grandfather said.

"Kashi's coming to the party too." Nick tried to keep his voice casual, as if he were talking about the weather. "How about I bring him up for a visit?"

"Hmm, okay," said Grandfather, putting on his earphones. "There's a rehash of last night's game coming on, and this afternoon I'm going to watch the Giants play the Redskins. Should be pretty good."

He flicked on the television set, and Nick knew it was time to leave.

That afternoon he waited impatiently on the veranda for Kashi. As soon as the tall, dark-haired figure came into sight, he rushed down the steps to meet him.

"Mrs. McHugh made something especially for you," he called.

"Then it must be blueberry cheesecake. I presume you're hoping I'll share?" Kashi took the steps two at a time, and Nick had to run to keep up with him.

Everyone else had arrived, including a middle-aged couple from town. Archie looked absent-minded, and he wore an orange tie with his green plaid jacket. Nick hadn't seen him around, but he'd heard the typewriter clicking, so the book must be going well. Tina, looking like a bumblebee in her yellow dress trimmed with black, buzzed around the room, laughing, teasing, explaining. Mrs. McHugh wore a long purple dress and gold bracelets. One of the bracelets was set with pearls and purple stones that matched her dress.

She extended a hand to Kashi, and he bowed over it. "What is this I hear about a marvelous blueberry cheese-cake?"

"Yes, indeed." Her gray eyes softened, and she led him to the table. As Nick followed, his elbow bumped a vase of dried flowers. It teetered toward the floor, and he grabbed it just in time.

"Good catch," whispered Robbie.

"Now that everyone has arrived," Mrs. McHugh said, "we may begin. Mr. Yoshimura, I will cut your cake."

It was fun having Kashi there, and the food was just as good as last Sunday's, but it seemed to Nick that the party would never end. He nibbled on a coconut cookie, hoping Kashi would remember about visiting Grandfather.

When Nick had eaten all he could, he filled a plate for Grandfather. The cheesecake, of course, and strawberries, and four tiny ham sandwiches. As he added a handful of cookies, he looked up to find Kashi standing beside him.

"For the grandfather?"

"Yes." Nick's heart took a quick, breathless leap, just thinking about it.

"I'm ready to go whenever you are." The cheerfulness in Kashi's voice was reassuring. Kashi carried Grandfather's glass of punch, and they climbed the stairs in silence. As they neared the door, Nick practiced what he was going to say. The usual two knocks, then—

But the doorknob would not turn. He checked the keyhole; it was dark, as if something were in it. A key?

He looked up at Kashi. "It's locked." His voice came out in a squeak. "He's locked the door."

He knocked again, louder this time. Maybe Grandfather had his earphones on—he'd be listening to the football game—and he hadn't heard. "Grandfather, it's me, Nick."

Silence flowed coldly from under the door. He couldn't even tell whether the television set was on because of the earphones. It didn't matter. He'd never locked the door before.

Slowly Nick turned away.

He paused on the landing, and Kashi waited beside him. The warm brown eyes were filled with sadness. "Give him a little more time, Nick; it's hard for older people to change. I think that God is not yet finished with your grandfather."

Nick tightened his grip on the plate and nodded, trying to swallow the ache in his throat. Kashi's hand rested lightly on his shoulder. "Save that plate of goodies for later on tonight. Perhaps you can use it as your coals of fire."

"Mr. Yoshimura!" Tina bounced into the hall. "I was looking for you. Archie needs a partner for chess."

Nick put the plate in the refrigerator and slipped out the back door. He wandered over to the grove of pine trees at the far end of the Inn and paced back and forth, closing his mind to everything but the murmuring wind in the trees. After a while he began to wonder what Kashi had meant by coals of fire. How could a plate of food—?

By the time he got back, the party was over. Good. He'd done enough smiling for today. He and Robbie started on the mountain of dishes. After they'd discussed their new kites, he asked his brother what people meant when they talked about "coals of fire."

Robbie looked puzzled. "Coals of fire? Oh, like in the Bible." He arranged a row of plates in the dishwasher. "There's a verse that says something about heaping coals of fire on your enemy's head. It means like . . . doing good things to someone who's been mean to you."

It still sounded odd to Nick. "Where's the verse?" he asked.

"I'm not sure, but I've got a concordance, so we can find it. You finished with those glasses? Okay, I'm done too. Let's go."

Nick sat on Robbie's bed while his brother looked up the verse. "Proverbs 25:22." Robbie gave him a curious glance. "What's this for? Doesn't sound like something you'd put in your project notebook."

"No, I was just wondering about it." Nick got to his feet. "But that's a good idea for my notebook. Thanks for checking." He wanted to look up the verse by himself.

As soon as he reached his room, Nick grabbed his Bible. He joined the little striped cat on his bed and found the twenty-fifth chapter of Proverbs without any trouble. Verses 21 and 22 went together. *If thine enemy be hungry, give him bread to eat; and if he be thirsty, give him water to drink: For thou shalt heap coals of fire upon his head, and the Lord shall reward thee.*

Was Grandfather his enemy? Sometimes, it seemed.

He knelt on his bed to look outside. The cat leaped onto the sill, but he didn't feel like opening the window. Kashi probably meant that he should take that plate of food up to Grandfather tonight and be as nice as ever. Act as if Grandfather hadn't broken his promise.

Nick leaned his forehead against the cold windowpane. How did Grandfather get that door locked, anyway?

At supper time, Nick hesitated in front of the door. Would it still be locked? No, the glass doorknob turned easily. Once inside, he glanced down at the keyhole. There was nothing in it.

"Here's your supper," he said as cheerfully as he could. "And . . . and I brought you some of Mrs. McHugh's very special junk food, from the party."

Grandfather was lying flat, his baseball cap covering most of his face. "Can't even take a nap without you people bothering me," he muttered.

But he sat up and pushed the cap back, just a little. "Junk food, huh?" He picked up a frosted strawberry and put the whole thing into his mouth. Then he licked the sugar off his fingers and started on the cheesecake. "Pretty good." He speared a blueberry with his fork. "Fresh blueberries. I can always tell."

"Yes," Nick said. "Mrs. McHugh made it especially for Kashi." He wanted to add, *and now Kashi knows that you're a grouchy old man who doesn't keep his promises.*

He bit his lip. "You said he could come see you. Why did you lock the door on us?"

The old man shot him a dark glance and took another bite. "Didn't feel like visitors." He pushed irritably at the tray, spilling his coffee. "That stuff is too rich. And my coffee is cold again. Can't you bring me some that's hot?"

He'd forgotten the Thermos. "Okay." Nick sighed inwardly. This coals-of-fire thing wasn't working out very well. He shouldn't have mentioned Kashi.

On his way down the stairs, he prayed, "Lord, what am I supposed to say to him?" He didn't get any good ideas, but by the time he returned, Grandfather had finished the plate of desserts and started on his meat loaf.

"How'd the Giants do today?" Nick asked.

"Good game. They won, of course. But you should have seen their defense." For the next ten minutes, Grandfather gave him a play-by-play account of the game.

While Nick ate supper, he thought up a coals-of-fire thing to say. He tried it when he picked up Grandfather's dishes. "I think it's great that you can get around on that broken leg. Do you have crutches, or did you do it the hard way when you locked the door?"

Grandfather looked surprised. "Well, there's crutches in the closet, but I didn't use them."

"When my friend Alex broke his leg, he hated his crutches," Nick said. "Then the doctor told him that his muscles would . . . what's that word—*atrophy*—if he didn't use them. Alex didn't want to be a cripple, so pretty soon he was going all over the place on those crutches." He paused. "I could help you with yours tomorrow."

Grandfather gazed at the ceiling; at least he wasn't fiddling with his earphones, like before. "Okay."

But would he do it? Without thinking, Nick said, "Do you really mean that, or are you going to change your mind?"

Now the old man looked straight at him, anger flaring in his dark eyes. He started to say something, then stopped and shifted his gaze. He pulled the quilt smooth, almost upsetting the tray. "I'm sorry, boy. I deserved that." He sighed. "Yes, let's try it."

Nick let out the breath he had been holding. "Okay." He picked up the tray. "I'd better take these dishes downstairs. See you tomorrow."

The next morning, Nick decided that getting back to normal wasn't all that bad. With Tina gone, everything seemed calmer. Just as he'd thought, there was a lot to vacuum in the dining room. While he worked, he wondered whether he and Robbie would get to fly their kites today, so he took a detour to look out the living room windows. The wind was still blowing hard, kicking up whitecaps on the waves.

He took Grandfather's lunch up to him and stepped to the bedroom window to check the weather for the twentieth time.

"What're you looking at?"

"I was hoping the wind would die down so we could fly our kites." He glanced at his grandfather. "After I help you practice with those crutches."

"If the wind is raising dust, then it's too strong," said Grandfather. "This afternoon will probably be all right unless it starts gusting." He stopped with his sandwich halfway to his mouth. "Why don't you go ahead and fly your kite, then come back and tell me how it went? We can crutch after supper."

Nick looked at him suspiciously. Was he trying to get out of walking? At least he was still agreeable. "Okay. I'll try to come back early."

They carried their kites down to the beach, even though Nick was still worried about the wind. "Do you think it's okay?" he asked Robbie.

"Yeah, maybe a little strong, but I've flown kites in worse than this."

Nick wished he could ask Kashi, but the man was working today. He wanted to tell Kashi about last night's talk with Grandfather too.

"What's the best way to start a kite flying?" he asked.

Robbie was busy doing something with his string. "See that string with the ring on it—remember Kashi called it the bridle?"

Nick took his kite by the bridle, as he'd seen Kashi do.

"Tie your string to that ring. That's your flying line."

"Okay."

Robbie turned his back to the wind. "Stand like this—" He held out his kite and the wind snatched at it, carrying it up into the air. He started after it. "Don't let the line out too fast," he called back. "This wind is picking up, so be careful." His kite climbed into the sky, looking like a huge, striped bird.

Nick held out his kite, hoping the string wouldn't get tangled. The kite quivered and seemed to come alive. It lifted into the sky, and Nick let the string slide through his fingers, just as Robbie had said. Soon it was high—almost as high as Robbie's. Its red spots stood out boldly against the white.

Looks like an alien being, he thought. I'll have to tell Archie.

"How do I make it go higher?" he called.

"Pull on the line a little," said Robbie. He turned to watch. "Yes, that's it."

A gust of wind sent Nick's kite skittering to one side.

"Run across the wind with it," Robbie yelled, "the same way it's going."

Nick ran down the beach, and the kite flew more steadily. My own creation, he thought, staring up at it. My very own.

The wind rose sharply, and another gust snapped the kite sideways. The flying line quivered, jerked, and then he felt an awful nothingness in his hand.

"My kite!" he cried. "Robbie, it's getting away!"

The kite dipped and twirled for a few seconds, then it began a long glide downward. It sailed toward the dunes, past the dunes, over the bayberry bushes.

"Maybe you can catch it," Robbie called. He was having trouble with his kite too.

Nick was already across the dunes and into the bushes. Just out of reach, the kite floated ahead of him. Somehow he found a path and ran down it, trying to follow the twists and turns and still keep track of the kite.

Slowly the kite dropped, then it disappeared from sight. It must have snagged on a bush. He scanned the expanse of twiggy gray branches. Yes! That looked like his string.

He left the path and plunged into the bushes. The spiny branches caught at his clothes and scratched his face, but he pushed on until he could see the string. Following it, he struggled from bush to bush toward a patch of white. His kite was impaled on a long gray branch that pointed to the sky.

It's a kite-eating bush, he thought, trying to cheer himself up. Just like in the cartoon.

He worked his way forward until he could grab the branch and bend it down. The cloth had torn a little, but he was so glad to have the kite back, he didn't mind. He pulled as much string as he could out of the bushes and wrapped it into a ball.

Now he had to figure out how to get back to the beach. The sun was setting, and he didn't have the faintest idea where he was.

He found a path and followed it until the ocean sounded nearby, but now he could hardly see in the twilight. He quickened his pace.

"Nicky? Nicky!" It was Robbie's voice, carried on the wind. "Where are you?"

"Here," he called back to the dark sky.

"Where are you?"

"Here!" If only he had a flashlight or something to signal with. Maybe his kite . . . He climbed up into a tall bush, then tied a string onto the kite's bridle. The wind snatched the kite out of his hands, carrying it straight up.

"Here—by the kite!" he yelled.

"I see it. Stay there."

When Robbie finally reached him, he carried a ball of kite string that unrolled behind him. "I sure am glad to see you," Nick said. "What's that for?"

"So we can find our way back." Robbie glanced at the path behind him. "Actually, we're not very far from the beach, but you'd never know it."

Before long, they were out of the bayberry bushes and heading toward the lights of the Inn. Nick's mother met them at the kitchen door. "I wondered where . . . Nicky! What happened to you?"

"I'm okay, Mom. Just a few scratches. My kite flew into the bushes."

"Looked to me like the knot on your flying line came loose," said Robbie.

All at once Nick felt dead tired; maybe he'd never take another step. He dropped into a kitchen chair. "Sorry I made us late. What can I do for supper?"

"It's all ready. Just wash up a bit, then you can take your grandfather's tray up to him." The buzzer rang imperiously, and she added, "Better hurry."

Grandfather! He'd promised to come back early and help him practice walking. Nick groaned.

8
Swing—Thump

Grandfather seemed to be in a good mood tonight. He chuckled at the sight of Nick's face. "Get into a fight, boy?"

Nick told him about losing the kite.

"That wind can be tricky this time of year. Why wasn't your friend there?"

"Kashi? He had to work—he's a retired pilot. Sometimes they call him when they need someone else to fly."

As soon as Grandfather finished, Nick took the tray downstairs, rushed through his own supper, and hurried back, hoping he hadn't changed his mind. "Where did you say the crutches are?" he asked.

"In the closet, I guess." Grandfather sagged against the pillows and slid the baseball cap down over his eyes.

Nick pretended not to notice. "Okay. You've got a walking cast, so this won't be so hard." He looked at the crutches, figuring out what to do next.

"These are pretty long—like the ones Alex had. His were too big for me, but I had fun with them anyway." He shot a glance at Grandfather. At least he was watching. "Let's see. Arms go there, hold on here, swing those crutches out, hop. Okay, I'm going to try it. Swing—*thump*. Swing—*thump*. Oops!" He stumbled, almost tripping over one crutch. "Try it again. Swing—*thump*. Guess I've got it."

He made a few trips up and down the room. "Now it's your turn."

Grandfather sat up slowly, and Nick chattered on. "Of course, you've got that bad leg—makes a difference. Just don't put your weight on it. Alex said it hurt something awful when he stepped on his leg."

"Yes. Alex was right." Grandfather sounded grim, but he had settled his baseball cap securely and swung his legs over the side of the bed.

"See if you can balance on your good leg—here, lean on me—and I'll get the crutches in the right place for you."

Grandfather was a lot taller than Nick had expected. Tall and skinny and a little stooped.

"There. Looks like they're the right height for you. Okay now, let's take it slowly." They started off. "Hey, you're good."

Grandfather stopped to rest. "It's easier than hopping on one leg and hanging onto everything."

So that's how he managed to lock the door, Nick thought. As Grandfather turned in a wavering circle, Nick remembered what Mom had said about brittle bones. What if he fell?

"That's enough for right now, okay?" Nick eased him back onto the bed. "We can do a little bit every day, and soon you'll be zooming all over the house."

"Says who?" Grandfather twitched the pillows behind himself and closed his eyes.

Nick thought of something else to say. "Remember you asked about the kites at Kashi's house?"

Grandfather's eyes opened, and Nick settled himself at the foot of the bed. "He made them—all of them. He learned how from his grandfather—he was a kite maker back in Japan."

"How many kites does he have?"

"Oh, lots—maybe a dozen, just on that wall. Some are real old."

"Has he ever been to Japan?"

"Kashi? I guess not."

"Hmm." Grandfather sounded tired, so Nick slipped off the bed and started for the door. "By the way," Grandfather murmured. "How's what's-his-name's book coming?"

"Archie's? I don't know. Probably okay."

"Too bad."

Nick stopped in the doorway. "What—?"

"Too bad someone doesn't have to cheer him up with another cake."

Nick had to grin at that. "Yeah, the party desserts are all gone, and Mom didn't get to do any baking today. See you tomorrow."

The next morning while they were fixing breakfast, Nick told his mother about helping Grandfather to practice walking. She gave him a big hug. "Nicky! That's wonderful. If he'll just get out of that bed, he'll feel so much better."

"He asked about Archie's book too," Nick said. "Sounded like he was hoping you would make another cake."

His mother finished stirring the pancake batter. "Why don't we make him something special to celebrate?" She glanced at Nick. "Or will he mind—"

"No, he'll like it as long as it's a good dessert. What's his favorite, do you know?"

"Lemon meringue pie, from scratch. How could I forget? It was your dad's favorite too. I used to make it for them all the time." She paused, then went on briskly, "Did you know that your grandfather is a good cook? It's really his recipe. Let's see now; do I have three eggs? Yes, and fresh lemons. I'll make it right after breakfast."

"Seems like Grandfather knows a lot of stuff," said Nick. "How come?"

"He used to cook at some famous restaurant, then he went back to school and became a science teacher," Mom said. She frowned at the pancakes in the frying pan. "Oh, no. Mrs. McHugh went into town for the morning, and I promised I'd give her rooms a thorough cleaning while she's gone."

"I'll help," said Nick. "I can get my other work done extra fast."

"Good. Maybe I'll have time, if I hurry. Peter's coming out today, so I've got to make lunch for him too."

Mrs. McHugh's parlor wasn't nearly as crowded as the last time Nick had seen it, but plastic peanuts littered the floor and everything seemed out of place, as though a whirlwind had come by.

His mother surveyed the room. "At least the driftwood creatures are gone," she said with a sigh. "Tina must have packed them up and taken them with her. Why don't you start vacuuming, then you can dust. Let's begin with the bedroom; it won't be so bad."

When they were almost finished, his mother left him to dust the parlor while she started making the pie. He was down on his hands and knees wiping the carved legs of the big round table when Mrs. McHugh walked into the room.

"What are you doing down there?" She sounded as though she'd caught him planting a bomb.

He backed out from under the table and held up the dust cloth like a badge. He wanted to say, *FBI, ma'am. Dusting for fingerprints,* but he resisted the temptation. "Dusting," he said.

"Why do you find that so amusing? Are you finished? I've got something to show you." She held an assortment of bags and a stack of books. He eyed them with curiosity and sped through the rest of the dusting while she put things away. She was standing there, watching him, by the time he got through.

She took some books from the ones she'd piled on the table. "I heard you talking about your school project. Sea gulls, isn't it?"

Before he could nod, she went on. "I was at the library getting some oceanography books for Archie—how that young man thinks he's going to write without doing research is beyond me—and I borrowed some books for you too."

She gave him three books, and Nick glanced at the top one. *Gulls Everywhere.* The others were *Gulls: Friend or Foe* and *Wings of the Sea.* "Hey, these look good!" He smiled, surprised that she had done this for him. "Thank you very much."

She waved away his thanks. "Here are two more, just for fun. I looked for *Kidnapped*, but it was checked out." She handed him *Treasure Island* and *The Book of King Arthur.* "Now don't get them dirty or leave them on the beach."

"Right." He started to carry them out of the room.

"Nicholas! Your dust cloth. And don't forget to shake all the dust outside."

"Yes, ma'am."

That afternoon, since the wind was still blowing hard, Nick decided to see if Kashi would help him fix his kite. "I'm coming too," said Robbie. "I want to try putting tassels on mine. Besides, I don't think I'm ever going to catch any fish."

Robbie phoned to see whether Kashi wanted visitors, then Nick gathered up his kite and the largest sea gull book. He hadn't seen Kashi since Sunday, and there was lots to tell him.

The smile lines around Kashi's dark eyes crinkled when Nick described how Grandfather had tried out the crutches. "I'm glad to hear that," he said.

They drank cocoa together, and as soon as Robbie was busy with his kite, Nick took the chance to speak privately with Kashi. "I tried the 'coals-of-fire' thing. I took the food back up to him, but I don't know whether it worked or not."

"Keep trying," Kashi said. "The idea behind that proverb is that God can use your kindness to bring the grandfather to repentance." He smiled at Nick.

Nick smiled back. He felt light inside, as though he could fly on the wind. That reminded him of the gulls and the library book. "Mrs. McHugh got a couple of books for me at the library. I brought this one to show you."

He waited while Kashi paged through *Wings of the Sea,* stopping occasionally to read a line or look at a picture.

"You'll find some good information here, and the photographs are excellent," Kashi said at last. "But when I see a book like this, it seems to me that something's missing."

"What do you mean?"

"They never mention the Creator who designed these beautiful birds."

"I guess a lot of people don't believe that God made everything," Nick said slowly.

"The first chapter of Genesis is true—no matter what anyone believes—and all of nature shows evidence of an intelligent Creator." Kashi turned to the chapter on gulls' wings. "See this diagram, how each feather has small barbs that connect it to the next one?" Nick studied the page, and Kashi added, "The Lord arranged it so the feathers lock together and protect sea birds from getting cold and wet. Details like this don't happen by accident."

He smiled and handed the book back to Nick. "Now tell me what happened to your kite, and we'll try to fix it."

They taped up the torn side of his kite, then Kashi explained how the weight of the tape would unbalance it, so Nick added an equal amount to the other side. In the meantime, Robbie had read about tassels in one of Kashi's books and made a set for himself out of yellow paper.

It was getting late when they started back to the Inn, and the cold, windy twilight reminded Nick of last night, when he'd chased his kite into the bushes. As they followed the path along the edge of a shallow gully, Nick watched the dark clouds massing overhead. "Yes, it certainly looks like we're in for a storm." He tried to say it the way Kashi had.

"Yeah." Robbie glanced at the book in Nick's arms. "I wish she'd brought me some books for my project."

"But you don't know what it is, yet."

"That's a problem." Robbie didn't say anything for a while. Finally he broke his stride to kick at shells on the path. "It's got to be something connected with the ocean, I guess. Now that Archie is into oceanography, maybe I'll talk to him. "

"You might get an idea," agreed Nick.

As they left the sheltering bushes, the full force of the wind struck them. Robbie gave a whoop that was lost in the thundering surf and broke into a run, with Nick close behind. By the time they reached the kitchen door, he was gasping for breath and his face tingled with cold.

Laughing together, they burst into the warm, fragrant kitchen. Supper tonight must be roast beef, Nick thought immediately. Nothing else could smell so good. "How's the pie doing?" he asked his mother.

She looked satisfied. "It's in the fridge. Put your things away, and then you can scrub some potatoes for me."

Later, as Nick carried the supper tray upstairs, he eyed the lemon meringue pie hungrily. Grandfather was really going to like this meal.

"Looks like you got some windburn today," his grandfather said.

"Yes, we went to Kashi's house to work on our kites. I patched mine and Robbie made tassels for his. Mrs. McHugh got me some books about sea gulls, so I took one to show Kashi . . ."

Grandfather didn't seem to be listening. He had picked up his fork and was staring at the pie. "Lemon meringue," he muttered. "What's she trying to do to me?" But he sank his fork into the glistening white meringue and sliced off a wedge of pie. He put the whole thing into his mouth without dropping a crumb. Then he closed his eyes, and his wrinkled old face looked both sad and angry. That worried Nick.

"Mom made it especially for you," he said. "I told her how you used your crutches, and she said we should celebrate."

"Huh." Grandfather opened his eyes and bent over the tray to carve off another bite of pie. He didn't look up.

"After supper I could show you those sea gull books," Nick said hurriedly. "And we can try walking some more." He edged toward the door. "See you later."

When his mother asked whether Grandfather had liked the pie, Nick didn't know what to say. "Well, he seemed sort of sad or something, but he sure ate it fast enough."

Robbie spoke up from the other side of the table. "Didn't you say it's his favorite? You surprised him, Mom. You threw the old buzzard a curve ball."

"Robbie, don't—he's your grandfather." Then Mom smiled a little. "But I did, I guess."

The pie was a coals-of-fire thing too, Nick decided silently.

That night, the storm brought pelting rain and wind that howled around the corners of the old house. Outside Nick's window, the pine tree creaked and groaned, banging its branches against the kitchen roof.

Nick paused over his notebook to wonder where sea gulls went to get away from a storm. He had almost finished his new page about gulls' wings when a thump made him look up at the ceiling.

Thump, then *thump,* then silence.

Nick grinned to himself. Swing—*thump.* He'd spent an hour with Grandfather after supper, and now the old man must be practicing some more. Good for him.

9
Secrets

The next morning it was still raining hard, but the wind had died, and it looked as if the storm was moving on. When Nick went out to sweep the windblown sand off the veranda, he found Archie pacing up and down. His hair seemed to be redder than the last time Nick had seen it, and extra curly.

"Finished with your book?" Nick asked, trying to remember what it was about.

Archie gave him a mournful glance. "How I wish! No, I started over again yesterday." He groaned. "I was thinking about having a sea creature in it, so Mrs. McHugh brought me some books from the library. Then I got the idea of making it underwater. You know—another whole civilization under the ocean. How's that sound?"

"Pretty good," Nick said cautiously.

"I thought so, too, but now I'm stuck." Archie turned toward the ocean with a sigh.

Nick wanted to ask whether he'd dyed his hair, and Archie must have felt him staring because he swung around. "Didn't get it quite right, did I?" he said, running a hand through his hair. Now it stood up in brilliant red corkscrews.

Nick pulled his gaze away with an effort and tried to think of something helpful. "What kind of creatures live underwater?" he asked. "And what kind of plants? Does it get hot and cold down there?"

Archie closed his eyes. "There's mountains and valleys on the ocean floor," he murmured.

"What about volcanoes?" Nick glanced down at the steps. They were too wet to sweep; he'd get them later.

Archie trailed behind him while he put away the broom and picked up a dust cloth, then headed for the living room. "I don't know," Archie muttered. "I just don't know enough."

Robbie looked up from where he knelt by the fireplace. "What don't you know, Archie?"

Archie slumped onto the sofa. He combed through his red curls with one hand, and Nick looked to see if it came away red, but it didn't. "I don't know enough about oceans," he said. "So how can I write my novel?"

"What about those books?" Robbie waved a hand at the stack on the coffee table.

Archie shook his head and fidgeted with a button on his cuff. "They gave me an idea," he said. "But now I've got to—"

He jerked upright. "Check it out! Museums. No . . . aquariums. Scuba diving. What's that place in Massachusetts called?" He thumbed through one of the books. "Woods Hole Oceanographic Institute." He jumped to his feet. "That's it. Where's your mother?"

"What's the matter, Archie?" Mom called from the kitchen.

"I'm off to do research, Mrs. Radford. Will you keep my room for me? I don't know how long—maybe a week."

Nick's mother came to the doorway. "Oh, can you be back for Tuesday?" She dropped her voice. "That's Mrs. McHugh's surprise birthday party. She'll be so disappointed if you're not here."

Archie was halfway to his bedroom. "Okay, I'll try to get back. Tuesday. Maybe I'll bring her something . . . " His voice faded as the door closed.

Robbie stood up from the fireplace, dusting off his hands. "Looks like I'm the only person around here without a project." He glanced out the window. "But the rain has stopped, and after lunch the tide will be right. Maybe I'll try two poles this time. Hey, Nicky, want to help me set them up?"

"Sure! I'll bring my kite too."

Nick had wondered how Robbie was going to manage two poles, but he figured it out when his brother pushed two metal tubes into the sand. "Tide's coming in," Robbie said. "I'll move them if I have to."

Nick put down the empty cooler he'd carried back and forth each day. "What're you fishing for?" He'd been meaning to ask.

"Bass, mostly, with chunks of clam for bait. But Peter said he's caught some flounder out here." Robbie stood a pole in one of the holders and handed the other pole to Nick. "We'll put two hooks on each pole and bait the bottom hook for flounder, just in case. Peter gave me some minnows to try."

While they were finishing, Mrs. McHugh strolled past with Chaucer trotting three paces ahead of her. His black fur was dripping wet, as if he'd just come out of the ocean. They were heading toward the point. Kashi must be feeding gulls over there, Nick thought, judging by their "here's food" cries.

"I'm going to take my kite over by Kashi," he said. He launched his kite, and by the time he rounded the point, it was flying steadily, climbing higher and higher. Kashi had finished with the gulls and stood talking to Mrs. McHugh.

As he drew near, she fixed her piercing gaze upon him. "How are those books serving you, lad?"

"They're great, Mrs. McHugh. I'm finding lots of information for my project."

"I thought they might be useful." She looked down the beach. "Well, we must be getting along. It has been pleasant visiting with you, Mr. Yoshimura."

"The pleasure was mine," he said in his courteous way. "Good hunting, Mrs. McHugh."

Hunting? Oh, the driftwood, Nick thought. "Want to see what the storm washed up last night?" he asked Kashi. "Maybe we can find some good stuff too." He'd given up on the treasure idea, but you never knew what a storm might uncover.

"Sure. I was going to take a walk anyway." Kashi headed for the dunes above the high-tide line, and Nick began reeling in his kite.

Today, the usual things were caught between the clumps of grass: bits of wood, pieces of frayed rope, a soda can, broken Styrofoam. Nick poked at the wide, flat shell of a stranded horseshoe crab and wrinkled his nose at its musty smell. He caught a glimpse of white behind a low dune. White feathers?

"Kashi!" He dropped his kite and ran to kneel beside a small gray-and-white bird. Kashi joined him an instant later.

"Is it dead?" Nick whispered.

"I don't know." Kashi touched the bird lightly, and Nick thought it moved a little. Or had the wind ruffled its feathers?

"What's the matter with it?" Nick couldn't see any blood.

Kashi spread one wing. It was a soft shade of gray, with black tips. "This looks okay, although it's lost some feathers." He lifted the other wing and the bird moved again. "Ah," said Kashi, "does that hurt?" He folded the wing back into place and turned the bird over. It lay still, eyes half-closed.

"Looks like a young bird; quite battered. Probably got caught in that storm last night and blown off course. Could have injured that wing."

"What kind is it?" Nick stroked the smooth white neck.

"An ocean-going gull called a kittiwake," said Kashi. "They usually fly far out over the water, and they nest in cliffs up north—in the Arctic and in Greenland."

"I've never seen one before."

"Sometimes we get them down here in winter. People call them frost gulls."

Nick felt a deep pity for the exhausted bird. She was all alone now, separated from her flock. "Do you think she'll live? Can we keep her? Maybe if I take good care of her, she'll get better and I can teach her tricks—"

"Not for a pet." Kashi stood to his feet. "It's not a good idea to take one of God's wild creatures and put it in a cage. Then someday you'll get tired of it and let it go, and it won't know how to live on its own."

"But maybe I could teach her how—"

Kashi shook his head, more somber than Nick had ever seen him. "After you've made it a pet, the bird will never be fit to live in the wild again. It would probably die right away."

"But we can't leave her here." Nick glanced down the beach. Sure enough, Mrs. McHugh was headed back this way. "Chaucer—or some other dog—will get her."

Kashi gazed down at the bird.

"Oh, look!" exclaimed Nick. The bird lifted her head from the sand, and her eyes fluttered open. They were round and dark, and very bright.

"We can find a quiet place for it to rest, if it doesn't die." Kashi gave Nick a stern glance. "Just until it's strong enough to fly, right?"

"Right." Nick bent over the bird as Kashi took her gently into his hand. She lay there unresisting, her eyes closed. Had she died already?

He picked up his kite, then hurried to keep up with Kashi's swift pace down the beach. As they turned onto the path through the dunes, he threw a glance over his shoulder. Mrs. McHugh and her dog had almost reached the place where the bird had fallen.

Kashi carried the bird into a small wooden shed next to his house. "We won't turn on a light," he said, "so it won't be frightened. Here, want to hold it? I'll fix up a box."

Kashi put the bird into Nick's hand. The small body was incredibly light and fragile—and warm. Under his fingers drummed the frantic beating of her heart.

Kashi pulled a cardboard box from under a workbench, punched holes in it with a screwdriver, and laid a folded cloth inside. He took the bird from Nick. "We'll put in a little bread and some water and leave it alone for a while."

The kittiwake lay motionless. Nick couldn't tell whether she was breathing or not, but when he started to worry, he remembered the beating heart. He pictured her fighting the wind that tore at her feathers, blinded by fog and rain, then falling exhausted on the beach. *Hang on,* he said silently, *you're safe now.*

"Can I phone you tonight and find out—" He couldn't say it, but Kashi understood.

"Sure. I'll check on the bird later. In fact, I'll phone and tell you how it's doing." As they left the shed, Kashi said, "Looks like the sun's setting. Your brother's going to wonder what happened to you."

"I'll hurry," Nick promised.

"Sure you know the way?"

"I think so." Nick spoke with more assurance than he felt, hoping that if he stayed on the main path, he'd be okay. He followed it down the edge of the gully, turned left when it turned, then stopped in puzzlement when it forked at a clump of grass with especially tall brown plumes. Left or right? It made sense to go left, toward the beach—okay. Before long, the path turned again; it seemed to be taking him away from the Inn. He trotted along it for a while, wishing he didn't have his kite to carry. No, this was definitely wrong.

I've got to get back to that fork, he thought. If I can find it. The sun was down below the bushes now, out of sight. Better run.

He almost missed the fork, but he remembered the clump of tall grass just in time, and swung to the right. Yes, this was the way.

When the path opened out onto the beach, he saw his brother crouched over something, down the shore toward the Inn. Nick ran as fast as he could, hoping Robbie hadn't noticed how late it was. He didn't want to tell about the kittiwake, not until he knew she would live.

Robbie had almost finished putting away his gear. He glanced up with a broad smile. "Look! I got a flounder." He held up a round, flat fish that he'd strung on a piece of rope.

"That's great!" The fish looked much like a sandy, brown-splotched dinner plate. "Are we going to have it for supper?"

"Hope so." Robbie swished the flounder in the ocean, then laid it carefully in the cooler. He thrust the poles into Nick's hands. "Here, want to carry these? I'll take the cooler." Nick juggled the poles and his kite as they hurried down the beach.

As soon as they reached the Inn, Robbie cleaned and filleted the flounder himself. "Good for you!" exclaimed his mother. "I'll fry it for supper."

Nick made sure that Grandfather got a piece, and he noticed that the old man ate it before his dessert, for once. When he came up to get the tray, he asked, "How'd you like Robbie's flounder?"

"Delicious," said Grandfather.

"I think it's the best fish I've ever eaten," said Nick. "Or else Mom's a really good cook."

"Your brother go fishing every day?"

"Just about. He was getting really discouraged because he didn't catch anything. He has to do a project like mine for school—only harder stuff—and I think he really wanted to write about something he'd caught."

"How's your project coming?"

"Okay." Nick hesitated. Should he tell Grandfather about the kittiwake? He glanced anxiously at the old man. "I found something today, but it's a secret."

The black eyes sparkled. "I like secrets. And I never tell."

Nick leaned closer. "We were walking on the beach, and we found a gull lying in the dunes. It was almost dead—from the storm, Kashi said. It's a kittiwake."

"What'd you do with it?"

"Put her in Kashi's shed. He said her wing is injured but maybe not broken. He won't let me make a pet of her, though. She's one of God's wild creatures and shouldn't be put in a cage."

"One of *God's* wild creatures?" Grandfather leaned back against the pillows and closed his eyes. At least he didn't tip his cap down.

Nick couldn't let that comment go unchallenged. "God made all the birds and animals. There's a verse in the Bible that says, *And God created every living creature that moveth.*"

Grandfather opened one eye. "You sure that's in the Bible? How'd you find a verse like that?"

"Yes; it's in Genesis, the first chapter," Nick said. "I wanted a verse to use with my project, and Kashi gave me an idea of where to look."

Grandfather closed his eyes again. "Might have known."

The phone rang and Nick jumped to his feet. "Kashi was going to call me—about the kittiwake."

"Come back and tell me."

Nick raced downstairs and almost ran into his mother at the bottom of the steps. "It's for you."

"Hi, Nick." Kashi sounded cheerful, and Nick's hopes rose. "The gull is still alive. It moved around some and even ate a little. Coming over to see me tomorrow? Bring your kite."

"Sure."

"Is everything all right?" asked his mother.

"Yes, everything's great!" Nick ran up the steps two at a time.

10

Just Tell the Truth

The next afternoon, Robbie was determined to catch another flounder. Nick helped him set up the poles, then he hurried to Kashi's house. The bird still lay quietly, and Nick thought her eyes didn't look as bright.

"Is she okay?"

For once Kashi didn't smile. "I don't think so. Won't drink. I don't know how much longer it can last without water."

Nick slid a finger across the bird's sleek back, and she did not move. *Don't die,* he told her silently. *We want to help you. What do you need?*

"Can't we do something?" he asked. "Maybe she doesn't like the kind of water we have down here. Maybe it tastes different. What kind of water is she used to?"

"You know, that gives me an idea," Kashi said slowly. "I've read that sea gulls can drink saltwater because they have a special pair of glands that remove the salt. Perhaps kittiwakes are more used to drinking seawater."

"Yes! I'll go get some."

"I'll come with you. Let's take this dish."

Nick wanted to run all the way to the ocean, but Kashi's long stride ate up the distance fast, and he had to trot to keep up with him. He prayed for the bird until they were out of the dunes and onto the beach.

Under a cloudy afternoon sky, the ocean lifted smooth gray swells, spreading placidly to the horizon. Kashi waded out a short distance to scoop up a dishful of the gray green water. Nick remembered how it tasted when he'd swallowed some by accident, and he couldn't imagine anyone wanting to drink the stuff. But if that's what you were used to . . .

When Kashi put the small dish of water beside it, the kittiwake lifted its head feebly but otherwise did not move. "Might be too weak by now," Kashi said. "Let's give it a taste."

He dribbled a few drops of seawater onto the bird's yellow bill and spoke to it in a low, crooning voice. "Maybe it's nervous, having us around. We'd better leave it alone for a while."

He stood up. "Want to fly kites?"

Nick knew he was trying to keep him from hanging around the gull all afternoon, so he agreed.

Today Kashi flew a kite that looked like a giant bug with black-and-yellow striped wings, a curving red mouth, and round black eyes. A cicada, Kashi told him.

He let Nick fly the red star kite, and when Nick saw the way its streamers rippled in the wind, he decided that it would be fun to build one of his own. He'd paint a bird in the center, maybe one that looked like the kittiwake.

While they watched the kites, Kashi told him kite stories. "Years ago, an engineer was trying to build a bridge over the Niagara River. It was a swift, rocky river, and ice floes made it impossible to send a boat across the gorge. He had all kinds of trouble until he offered ten dollars to anyone who could fly a kite to the other side. One boy managed to fly his kite to men on the opposite bank, and then the engineer attached a rope to the kite string and used that rope to haul larger ropes and cables across."

Kashi also told him how scientists used to send their weather instruments up into the clouds by means of kites, and photographers sent up cameras to take aerial photographs.

It was fun, flying the kites and listening to Kashi, but Nick couldn't forget the dying kittiwake. Finally he asked, "Do you think she's taken a drink by now?"

"Hope so. Let's go see."

The shed seemed much too quiet as they stepped inside. Then Nick heard a scratching sound that made his heart leap. The kittiwake was standing up, looking very much alive and watching his every move. "She drank some!" Nick gazed happily at the dish of seawater.

A smile lit Kashi's dark eyes. "That's what it needed."

"Now you get well," Nick said to the bird, using the same crooning voice that Kashi had. "Get well and you can fly around and have fun again."

Later, walking back to the Inn with Robbie, Nick decided that it had been a pretty good afternoon. He whistled softly to himself, remembering. The kittiwake was better. Kashi had let him borrow two sea gull books. And his brother had caught another flounder, a larger one.

Robbie was full of enthusiastic plans for his project. "A flounder has both eyes on the same side of the head," he told Nick. "That's so it can lie flat on the bottom of the ocean and then leap up to catch smaller fish or whatever goes by."

"Sounds like you've been reading those books of Archie's."

"Yep. One book said that at first the eyes are in the regular place, but when the flounder matures, one eye moves so they're both on the same side of its head. There's more stuff too. I'm going to keep all the bones from this flounder and try to reconstruct the skeleton." Robbie talked all the way to the Inn.

Nick's mother cooked the flounder another way this time—baked in sauce—and Nick and Grandfather agreed that it tasted just as good as yesterday's. When Nick came up to get his supper dishes, Grandfather asked, "How's your sea gull doing?"

"We thought she was going to die because she wasn't drinking anything. Then Kashi got the idea of giving her saltwater, and she seems to be better."

"Saltwater, eh? Whose cicada kite was flying today?"

"Oh, the giant bug? That's Kashi's. You should see it up close." He stopped. "Do the Japanese eat cicadas too?"

Grandfather shook his head, and he might have been smiling. "No, they just like to listen to them. You've probably heard cicadas yourself, in the summertime."

"They must fly kites a lot in Japan."

"They do," said Grandfather. "They used to fly kites to celebrate the emperor's birthday. They still fly kites when a baby boy is born. And every spring they hold kite festivals. But I liked the kite fighting."

"They fight each other with kites?"

"Not exactly. It's more like a contest to see whose kite can stay up the longest. Maybe they have some way of cutting each other's kite strings. Your Japanese friend could probably tell you."

Nick heard the undercurrent of something—dislike?—in Grandfather's voice, and he tried to ignore it. "So now you're getting around all right by yourself?" Grandfather must have been up at the window this afternoon, watching the kites.

"I'll show you." He swung his legs over the edge of the bed, balanced for a minute on the crutches, then slowly thumped across the room.

"Hey, you're better than ever."

Grandfather took two more trips the length of the room. His arms trembled with the effort. Nick could see that he was tiring. "Guess I'll get back to bed while I'm still in one piece," he said finally, and lowered himself onto the quilt. "Sure is a hard way to get around."

He turned on the TV set, and Nick remembered that he'd come up for the tray. He was supposed to be doing dishes tonight too. Grandfather gave him an absent-minded wave as he left.

Mrs. McHugh walked into the kitchen while Nick was still loading the dishwasher. "Nicholas," she said abruptly, "do you ever go into my room?"

He glanced up, surprised. "Sometimes, to help Mom clean."

"What kind of cleaning do you do?"

"Mostly vacuuming and dusting." He put in the basket of silverware and straightened up. What was the matter with her?

"Do you ever go in there by yourself, just to look around?"

"No." He tried to remember the last time he'd dusted her parlor. Maybe he'd forgotten that table in the corner. It was Tuesday, the day Mom had made the pie for Grandfather, and he'd been in a hurry.

"Nicholas, look at me when I speak to you."

"Yes, ma'am." Her eyes were like splinters of gray ice.

The back door opened, and Robbie stumbled into the kitchen with an armful of firewood. "Nicky, get another load for me, will you?"

"Sure." Nick hurried outside, and when he returned with the wood, Mrs. McHugh was gone.

He tried not to think about her for the rest of the evening, but even when he was describing the kittiwake for his notebook, he could see her cold eyes. They looked so . . . suspicious. What was going on?

The next morning Mrs. McHugh took Mom into her parlor and talked to her with the door shut. Nick went on with his chores. After a long time, Mom walked into the living room. Her face was pale and her eyes were glittering like they did when she was upset.

"Nicky," she said, "Mrs. McHugh wants to talk to you. In here."

The old lady wore the same stony expression as yesterday. She and his mother sat down, but he stayed on his feet.

"Now, lad, just tell me the truth, here in front of your mother."

Nick waited. It always meant trouble when they said "just tell the truth."

"Have you ever come into my bedroom for some purpose other than cleaning?"

"No." He frowned, thinking. He was sure of that, at least.

"Nevertheless, you have been in my bedroom this week?"

"Yes, but—"

"To help your mother. I know, that's what you said."

It sounded suspicious, the way she put it.

"Did you take anything out of my bedroom?"

"No!" So that's what it was. He felt his cheeks redden with indignation, and he made himself look straight at her.

Her eyes bored into him, and he felt unaccountably guilty. "What's going on? I didn't take anything." He threw an imploring glance at his mother.

"I know you didn't," Mom said, and he could breathe again. "Mrs. McHugh can't seem to find one of her bracelets—the amethyst one."

He wondered what was important about "amethyst," but she was already talking. "It has purple stones in it, and pearls. Have you seen it around anywhere?"

"She wore it at the Tea," he said. "No, I haven't seen it lately." He glanced at her bony wrist, at the four silver bangles she wore today. Had she noticed how he always looked at her bracelets?

His mother stood up. "This is ridiculous, Mrs. McHugh. Accusing an innocent boy isn't going to get your bracelet back. Thank you, Nicky. Go ahead and finish the living room."

In spite of what his mother had said, Nick wondered about it for the rest of the morning. That woman really thought he had stolen her bracelet. Why did she think he was that kind of kid?

At lunch time he made himself a sandwich and took it up to his room. "I'm going to work on my project this afternoon," he told Robbie. "Maybe I'll come down to the beach later on." The last thing he wanted to do was run into Mrs. McHugh— anywhere.

He pried his window open and sat there, letting the cold, salty air wash over him. The little striped cat appeared and sniffed delicately at his sandwich, so he broke off a corner of bread for her. "Here you are, Short Stuff." He ate the rest slowly, watching the pine branches stir. Behind them, the sky was deep blue, laced with high clouds. He wished he'd thought to pick up some cookies.

As he worked on his notebook, he kept stopping to listen. The cries of distant gulls came to him on the breeze, and the slow beat of the sea filled his ears. The tide must be coming in. The little sandpipers would be dashing just ahead of the waves; the gulls would be circling around Kashi's head. The kittiwake! He'd almost forgotten about her.

He jumped up, started for the door, then stopped. What if he ran into Mrs. McHugh at the foot of the stairs?

He wandered back over to his window. If only there were some other way . . . Of course—the tree. He'd been meaning to climb it, anyway. He leaned out over the sill, thinking that the roof looked pretty dry. One of those long branches hanging across it ought to hold his weight.

His sneakers gave him good traction on the roof, and he avoided the dead part of the tree, choosing a thick branch that took him to the trunk. From there he went down, hand over hand, from branch to branch. The cat had followed him into the tree, but she stayed by the roof, watching his progress.

Halfway down, he paused to get his breath and realized that he was just outside the kitchen window. Mrs. McHugh stood there, looking out. She saw him. He was sure of it, for she turned and said something to his mother.

Nick slid down the rest of the way so fast that he scraped his hands on the rough bark. Mrs. McHugh would think it was sneaky for him to leave his room by way of a tree. Just the kind of thing a thief would do. He dropped the last few feet to the ground, picked himself up in a hurry, and ducked into the clump of pines at the end of the Inn.

He found Kashi on the beach talking to Robbie. His brother had set up two poles again. Kashi greeted Nick with a smile. "I wondered whether you were coming today."

Nick scrubbed at the pine pitch on his hands and tried to forget Mrs. McHugh. Had Kashi told Robbie about the kittiwake? He hoped not. At least, not yet. "Want to go for a walk?" he said.

"Sure." Kashi swung into his long, easy stride, and Nick trotted beside him. As soon as they were a safe distance down the beach, Nick asked, "How is the kittiwake?"

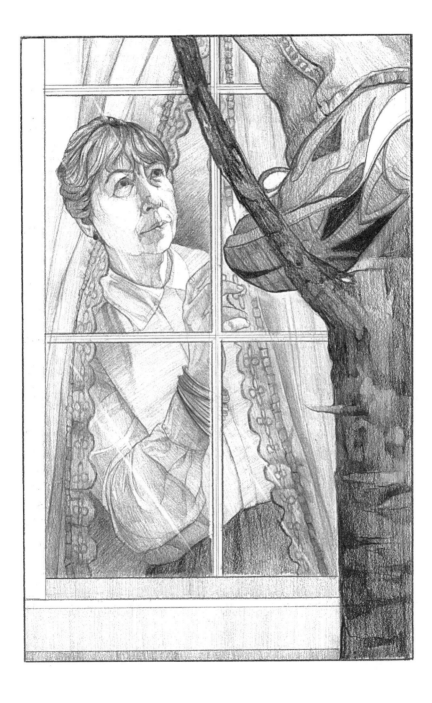

"Doing better. Eating and drinking, just the way it should. Come and see for yourself."

That evening, Nick gave Grandfather a full report. "She was walking around all over in the box. Maybe we'll have to get a bigger box. I held out some bread, and she gobbled it down. Did you know that sea gulls will eat just about anything?"

"That's for sure," Grandfather said.

"And while we were cleaning out the box, she walked all over Kashi's workbench, but she didn't try to fly. She's got the brightest eyes, and she turns her head to watch us, like she knows we're friends." Nick paused for breath. "I wish you could see her."

Just then, he noticed that Grandfather wasn't wearing his pajamas; he'd put on sweatpants and a Cardinals sweatshirt that hung loosely on his narrow shoulders. "Hey, you're all dressed up—looks good! How's the walking coming?"

"Not so bad. The doctor was here this afternoon. Said I'm doing better. Told me to keep exercising."

"Well, maybe you and I can get out to see the kittiwake sometime soon. Kashi let me borrow some of his books. I'll show you—one of them has a picture that looks just like her."

Nick ran down to his room and brought up all his sea gull books. Then he stayed late while they watched a football game together on the small television set.

Next morning, he slept in as long as he could. After all, this was Saturday. Drowsily he stared through the window. At home, he might have played baseball today with some of his friends. Or gone for a bike ride with Alex. He certainly wouldn't be spending half the day cleaning house—and doing an extra good job because of Mrs. McHugh's tea party tomorrow.

Mrs. McHugh. The memory of yesterday jerked him wide awake. He'd had about all he could take of her. That old . . . he searched for a word to describe her, one that was bad enough. That old . . . *gryphon*. He'd seen a drawing of the fierce creature in the King Arthur book, and it suited her perfectly.

A herring gull flew into the tree, closely pursued by another, and they squabbled there with petulant, screeching cries. Nick rolled out of bed, feeling tired. What right did she have to accuse him of taking that bracelet? And what could have happened to it, anyway?

Slowly he began to get dressed, trying to think of a solution. He'd read a story once about a crow that stole shiny things. But Mrs. McHugh never left her windows open, and besides, this bracelet was too heavy. He could picture it clearly: the wide gold band, the sparkling purple stones with pearls between. Pack rats took shiny things too.

He shook his head. No pack rat would dare to set foot in Mrs. McHugh's bedroom.

Now, if this were a Hemming Brothers mystery, what would *they* do? He stopped in the middle of tying one sneaker. They'd *find* the bracelet and prove their innocence. But how could he . . .

What if it weren't stolen at all? What if it were lost? Old ladies—old gryphons—forgot things sometimes. Maybe it had fallen behind her dresser. Shane Hemming would get into that bedroom somehow and find it, that's for sure. Why couldn't he?

"Hey, Short Stuff—you up yet?" Robbie swatted the door as he went past.

"Sure am. Coming." Nick pulled on his other sneaker, tied it, and followed Robbie down the stairs. Mrs. McHugh had said she was going into town this morning, so at least he didn't have to worry about running into her.

By the time breakfast was over, he'd made up his mind. Mom had talked to him, telling him not to worry, but he was still determined to find that bracelet.

"How come you're so quiet?" Robbie asked.

"Oh, just thinking." After he'd found the bracelet and it was all over, he'd tell Robbie and they'd have a good laugh. But for now, he had to be careful. The Hemming Brothers never told anyone their plans.

gryphon

11
A Shortcut

This morning Nick chose the window-washing job he'd been putting off; he'd start in the living room. That way he could pick just the right moment to check out Mrs. McHugh's rooms. His chance came when Robbie left to do the upstairs bathrooms and Mom took some laundry upstairs.

He slipped into Mrs. McHugh's parlor, closing the door quietly behind him, and began searching at one end of the room. Methodically he crawled from table to table, moving chairs, ducking under tablecloths, peering around stacked books. He found a narrow space behind her small writing desk and eased it away from the wall. Something fell onto the rug with a soft thud. He pushed the desk out farther, sending books and papers to the floor, but that didn't matter. Eagerly he reached for the object on the rug. A stapler. He tossed it onto the desk, feeling sweaty now, and began to pick up the books.

Voices reached him from the kitchen. Mom and—Peter? No. Not Mrs. McHugh! She'd come back early. "Stay there and talk, *please,*" he muttered. In desperate haste, he snatched up the last of the books.

"Nicholas!" She stood in the doorway, staring at him.

He wanted to run, but his legs wouldn't move. She advanced into the room, her eyes darting into every corner. He got to his feet and edged toward the door.

She frowned in puzzlement. "What are you doing in here?" Then her voice changed. "Did you decide to put it back?"

He groaned inside. Wordless, he shook his head.

"Just give it to me, and everything will be all right."

Finally he choked out something. "I didn't take it." He ducked past her and flew upstairs to his room.

A minute later, his mother knocked at the door. "Nicky, what's the matter? Are you sick?"

"Come in, Mom." He'd have to tell her all about his plan. It didn't seem so smart anymore.

After she left, he stayed in his room and tried to concentrate on schoolwork. The next thing he knew, Robbie was at his door. Then he had to explain everything to Robbie because Robbie had heard Mom talking to Mrs. McHugh. When he finished, Robbie looked at him in amazement. "Boy, that was sure stupid."

"I know, I know. But it sounded like a good idea." He decided not to say anything about the Hemming Brothers. "Hey, would you ask Mom if I can finish the windows this afternoon when Mrs. McHugh goes to the beach?" He rolled over on his bed, avoiding his brother's gaze. "I just want to keep out of Mrs. McHugh's way. I hate the way she looks at me." And I hate her, too, he added silently.

"Yeah, okay. Poor kid. I sure wouldn't want to be in your shoes." Robbie paused at the door. "I'll tell you when she leaves."

His brother went off, whistling, and Nick tried to get interested in *Treasure Island*. When Robbie called from downstairs, he slipped out to the hall window and checked the beach. Yes, the old gryphon was there, almost as far down as the point. She was probably looking for Kashi, to tell him the whole story.

He ate a quick lunch and set to work finishing the living room windows. Peter had come to fix something on the roof, and he was talking to Mom and Robbie out on the veranda. After they discussed the flounder Robbie had caught, the conversation turned to the weather.

"It's been pretty quiet so far," said Peter, "but you can bet we'll have a couple of bad storms this winter. Sometimes I worry about Miss Margo out here in this old house."

He waved toward the beach. "Used to be two big old pine trees out there, but they came down in that hurricane. If I were her, I'd take the hint and cut down the one by the kitchen too. But she says her daddy planted that tree and she can't bear to touch it."

While Peter went on talking, Nick thought about how glad he was that the old pine tree hadn't been cut down. Then he caught sight of Mrs. McHugh; she had almost reached the steps below the veranda. He gave the window one last swipe, put away the bottle of window cleaner, and escaped to his room.

Treasure Island was getting pretty exciting, and he had the striped cat for company. The afternoon went quickly, except for the times when he stopped to wonder how the kittiwake was doing and what Mrs. McHugh had said to Kashi.

With Robbie's help he managed to avoid her all evening, and he went to bed early. Praying seemed like too much trouble. He skipped it and fell asleep right away.

Sunday morning he woke up with a headache. For a while he hoped he was sick. Then he wouldn't have to go to the Tea this afternoon. Robbie had told him the food would be especially good because some ladies from town were coming, but even that didn't help. The thought of sitting in the gryphon's parlor, pretending that everything was just fine, made his stomach lurch. She would look at him with those eyes. And Kashi would be there.

He dragged himself out of bed. Until they found the bracelet, he wanted to stay away from everybody. It *had* to be in her bedroom. He should have checked there first.

The headache had disappeared by the time they met in Mom's bedroom for their worship service, but he didn't feel any better.

On the sermon tape, the speaker talked about how sin could separate a Christian from God. "Do you know of something in your life that's not right?" he asked. "It's probably making you miserable. Listen! You can't change it by yourself, but God can, if you ask Him."

Nick's attention fastened on the word *change.* That was what he wanted for Grandfather. He listened for a while more, but then his mind began to wander, and all he could see was Mrs. McHugh's face. During prayer time he found himself worrying about the party again, and he tried to pray about it. There had to be some way he could get out of going.

Then, while he was helping in the kitchen before lunch, he got an idea. His mother was talking about party food for Grandfather: "Be sure to get him one of those lemon tarts—"

"Mom, could I skip the party and spend the time with Grandfather?"

She looked up from the plate of cookies she was arranging. "I don't see why not. It might be crowded in there, today." She sighed. "I can't imagine where that bracelet could be. I helped Mrs. McHugh look all over her bedroom yesterday."

Not in the bedroom? He'd been counting on that. "It's got to be somewhere," he muttered. Tears burned at the back of his eyes, and if he were just a little younger, he would have let them come. "It seems like I'm always causing trouble for you. I wanted to help . . ."

She put an arm around him. "Don't you worry about it! The truth will come out eventually. And you *are* a help to me. Just let the Lord take care of it; He knows what's in your heart." She paused. "But promise me that you won't go back into Mrs. McHugh's rooms, no matter what."

He sighed. "Yes, I've decided that for sure."

That afternoon, Grandfather looked surprised when Nick brought up some extra food and sat in his usual place at the foot of the bed.

"Skipping out on the grand tea party?"

Nick looked down at his plate. He didn't feel like eating any of it. "Well, yes." Then he told Grandfather about the missing bracelet and how he'd tried to find it and ended up in more trouble. "The worst part about the Tea is that Kashi will be there, and she'll tell him all about it, if she hasn't already. They're old friends—he'll probably agree with her that I took it."

Grandfather stopped chewing. "From what you've said about him, I don't think he'll judge you guilty just because she says so. Did I ever tell you about the time when I was in boot camp and my buddy and I got thrown into jail?" Nick shook his head, and Grandfather took a big bite of cake. "We'd pulled a few pranks—"

He launched into a long story from his Air Force days, and by the time he finished, the knot in Nick's stomach had eased. He was licking fudge sauce off his fingers when Grandfather hoisted himself onto his crutches and hobbled to the window. "So what's new out there today?"

Nick joined him, looking for Kashi's house in the wilderness of bushes. There it was, with the weathervane standing still for once. "You know," he said, half to himself, "there's got to be a shorter way to get to Kashi's house. It doesn't look very far, but it sure takes a while to get there."

"How do you usually go?"

"Down the beach around the point, then we take a path behind the dunes." He glanced at his grandfather. "There's a couple of different paths through there. Maybe I could find one that leads to the back of the Inn."

Grandfather sat down on the window seat. "Won't know till you try, will you?"

"You mean—go now?"

"Why not? The McDragon will be at her tea party for a while longer, so you don't have to worry about her. Weather looks good." He gave Nick one of his rare smiles. "I'll call out the Coast Guard if you don't come back in a day or two."

"Yeah," Nick said. "I almost got lost in there once. Must be something I can do. Maybe some kite string . . ."

Grandfather raised an inquiring eyebrow, and Nick explained. "I should tie something to the bushes so I can find my way back."

"Blaze the trail, huh?"

"Sort of." Nick's idea improved as he talked. "I've got some cloth left over from making my kite. I could tear it into strips." He started for the door.

"Take a snack for the kittiwake, with my compliments." Grandfather wrapped one of Mrs. McHugh's dainty sandwiches in a napkin and handed it to Nick.

"Thanks! See you later."

It didn't take a minute to pick up the cloth and a jacket from his room, but getting out of the house was a different matter. He'd have to use the tree and hope that no one was in the kitchen.

Once safely down the tree, he began looking for a path through the bushes beside the Inn. Finally he discovered one. It was faint, but it seemed to lead in the right direction. He followed it, tying strips of cloth to branches as he went, and found that it skirted the edge of a wide, shallow gully. When it disappeared, he picked it up again on the other side of the gully.

Before long he came to a fork that seemed familiar. Those tall plumes of beach grass—was it the clump he always looked for? He tied a strip of cloth there, and turned onto the path that should lead to Kashi's house. A minute later he could see the weathervane ahead of him, and he ran the rest of the way in triumph.

Inside the shed it was dim, but Nick kept the light off. He discovered that Kashi had moved the kittiwake into a larger box covered with wire netting. On the box was taped a note: *Nick, please feed me.* Kashi must have known he would come for a visit.

The bird's dark eyes looked watchful, but she didn't move away when he knelt close to the box and spoke to her in the low, crooning voice Kashi used. "Brought you a present," he said, "with Grandfather's compliments." He tore up Mrs. McHugh's sandwich and dropped it through the wire, piece by piece. The kittiwake deftly caught each one.

"Hey, you were hungry, weren't you?" He slipped a hand under the wire to put grain in her food dish, then he ventured to stroke her tail feathers. She didn't seem to mind. "Gotta leave now," he said. "It's getting late. I'll come back as soon as I can."

Outside the shed, he took a quick look around and decided that Kashi must still be at the party. But what if he's on his way back, he thought. What if I meet him on the path? He might ask me—

Nick took off down the path at top speed, making sure he turned the right way at the clump of grass. He backtracked along his shortcut, following the cloth strips. As he drew closer to the Inn, he wondered whether Grandfather was watching from his window. He jumped up and down, waving the rest of the cloth, just in case.

The kitchen light was on, but the shade was down. He took his time about swinging himself up into the tree and over the edge of the roof. From there it was easy to climb through his window. Grandfather was back in bed, but he took off his earphones to listen to Nick's report. "Sounds like your expedition was a success. When're you going to let that bird go free?"

Nick had been thinking about that. "Soon, I guess. Wish you could see her."

Grandfather started to put his earphones back on, then he said, "If wishes were horses, beggars would ride."

Nick knew what he meant, sort of, but he still didn't want to give up on his idea. It would be good for Grandfather to get out—and then he'd meet Kashi too.

Sometime in the middle of the night, Nick woke up, wondering again how he could get Grandfather over to see the kittiwake. He could ask Kashi—he might even offer Grandfather a ride. But if Mrs. McHugh had convinced Kashi that Nick was a thief, he probably wouldn't want him around at all. Nick pushed the thought away and sat up in bed to rearrange his pillow.

Before he knew it, he was worrying about the bracelet again. It *had* to be somewhere in the Inn. No one would have taken it. Would they? He made a list in his mind and checked off the name of each suspect, like the Hemming Brothers did. Not Grandfather. Not Mom. Not Robbie. Certainly not Peter—he hadn't even been here that weekend. Not Kashi;

he'd only come last Sunday for the Tea, and Mrs. McHugh was wearing the bracelet that day. Who else was there? Archie had left on Wednesday. When had she missed the bracelet? Thursday.

Archie? He didn't want it to be Archie. But Archie's room was right next to hers, and he certainly had been in a hurry to leave. Could he have taken it with him?

Drowsily Nick considered the idea. He didn't know what to think about Archie. A guy who dyed his hair might be capable of anything.

He yawned. Before he went back to sleep, he'd better pray for Grandfather—he'd forgotten to do that last night. But when he tried to pray, Mrs. McHugh's face was all that came into his mind, and with it, a thrust of cold dislike. The old gryphon. He rolled over, jerking the blankets with him and dislodging the cat. She scrambled for a more secure place and stood there, watching him.

What was the matter? Why couldn't he pray? He hadn't felt like this since the time he'd told Mom that lie about Robbie. He sighed. Okay, so he shouldn't be hating Mrs. McHugh; he knew that. But she'd been so—

"It's not fair, Lord. I can't help hating her," he whispered into his pillow. Then he remembered the sermon tape from Sunday. "But I don't want to be separated from You, Lord. I'm *sorry*. Please change the way I feel about her—I know You can . . . " He waited, but all he felt was renewed concern for Grandfather. "And change Grandfather's heart—he really needs You badly—and Lord, I don't know what to do about that bracelet." Now the words came freely, and he poured out his fears.

After he'd finished, he reached for the cat, who was sitting warily at the foot of his bed. "We can sleep now, Short Stuff," he said, and she nestled close beside him.

He dreamed about the kittiwake. She was flying off over the ocean, strong at last, and he knew he'd never see her again.

Remembering the dream—and his plan to take Grandfather to see the kittiwake—gave him the courage to phone Kashi the next morning. There was no answer. As Nick was hanging up the phone, Robbie asked, "Who're you calling?"

"Kashi. He's out, I guess."

"Yeah, he's working. He told me on Saturday he had a long flight this weekend and wouldn't be back until tonight."

"Oh." Nick thought about that. "He wasn't at the Tea yesterday?"

"Nope. But I guess he knows about Mrs. McHugh's birthday bash tomorrow. Said he'd make sure he's back for it."

"Okay." Nick started his chores with plenty to think about. Kashi hadn't been here yesterday, but he'd known that Nick would come over to see the kittiwake. That explained the note. What about Grandfather? With Kashi gone, it didn't make much sense to try to get Grandfather over there.

He went out onto the veranda to shake his mop and watched the gulls drifting high over the ocean. What if he brought the kittiwake to Grandfather? Mom wouldn't mind, just for a visit. And he'd be careful to stay away from Mrs. McHugh. He twirled the mop in clever spirals through the air. Oddly enough, he didn't feel like calling her an old gryphon anymore.

After lunch, when he went up to get Grandfather's tray, he asked, "Are you going to take a nap this afternoon?"

"Of course I am. I always take a nap." Grandfather settled the baseball cap over his eyes. "Starting now."

"Okay." Nick almost said something about bringing him a visitor, then decided not to. He closed the door softly behind him.

12
The Kittiwake

The first thing he had to do was find out where Mrs. McHugh was. At this time of day, she might be anywhere in the Inn. Too bad she didn't take naps. Well, he had to help with the dishes no matter what.

As soon as he finished in the kitchen, Nick slipped out the back door. His shortcut to Kashi's house was easy to find, and on the way he stopped a few times to tie the fluttering cloth strips more securely.

The kittiwake was glad to see him, he was sure of it. She looked up when he walked into the shed, then hopped up and down in the box with short, excited squawks. Maybe she could tell that he'd brought food: some leftover toast and a small can of clams from the pantry. He took the wire top off the cage so she could practice flying, and while he was opening the clams, she fluttered up onto the workbench.

"You're sure getting lively," he said. "Here, want a bite to eat?" He tossed pieces of toast into the air for her to catch, and then put her back in the box so she could eat the clams. After he'd filled her water dish from the jug of seawater, he sat and talked to her. The bird was preening her plumage, nibbling and poking at her feathers, gently chewing them and drawing them through her beak. She worked from one side of her body to the other, arranging the feathers into a smooth cover.

It took her a long time, and Nick wondered why she bothered. He'd seen gulls on the beach preen their feathers too. That would be a good thing for his notebook.

"Well, now, you're all ready to go visiting," he said, getting to his feet. He looked at the box. It was too big to carry all the way to the Inn. How about something smaller? While he was searching, the kittiwake fluttered past him and landed on the workbench again. He reached for her, and she flapped off to the other side of the shed. "Looks like we need a box with a top," he said, but he couldn't find anything that would work.

The gull was back on the workbench, preening again. He watched her absently, trying to think what to do. If Mrs. McHugh was around, he'd have to climb the tree in order to get inside. How could he manage a box, anyway?

His gaze fell on an old towel under the workbench. What if he used that? —Yes!

The bird didn't seem to mind when he wrapped the towel snugly around her small body, immobilizing her wings. Then, remembering the sharp beak, he loosely covered her head too. A moment later, they were out the door and down the path.

When he reached the Inn, Nick hesitated. He could hear voices from the veranda, so Mrs. McHugh was probably out there. He'd better climb the tree. After a moment's thought, he unzipped his jacket, unbuttoned the top of his shirt, and slid the bird inside. She made no sound, but he had forgotten about her feet; they scrabbled and scratched against his skin.

"It won't be long," he whispered as he tucked in his shirt. That seemed to make the bird feel more secure, for she stopped struggling. He zipped up his jacket and swung into the tree.

Halfway up, he began to worry about his window. He always left it propped open, but what if someone had closed it? He craned his neck to see. Good, his stick was still in place. The gull was beginning to squirm loose, and by the time he reached the roof, she had poked her head out of his jacket. Quickly he crossed the roof, and then, afraid of crushing the gull, took her out and held her in one hand while he hoisted himself over the sill.

"Here we are!" He eased onto the bed, laughing with relief.

The cat leaped up from his pillow and scrambled to the foot of the bed. She watched the bird narrowly, her tail twitching.

Nick grinned at the cat. "This is a kittiwake. Bigger than you are, isn't she? Just mind your manners and nobody will get hurt." The bird turned her head toward the sound of his voice and didn't seem to notice the cat.

"Have you ever seen a grandfather?" Nick whispered, holding the bird close. "Maybe not, but c'mon, let's go." Carefully he put her back inside his jacket. "Just for a minute."

Grandfather was sitting up in bed, reading. "Thought you'd gone to the beach," he said.

"Well, I did, sort of. I brought someone to see you." Nick sat down and took out the gull. After he'd unwrapped her, she found her footing on the quilt and shook out her feathers.

Grandfather leaned forward. "The kittiwake!"

The gull cocked her head, surveyed the room, then launched herself with a flurry of wings. She circled the room and landed on a bedpost across from Nick.

"See how well she flies?" Nick felt as if he'd just made a successful flight himself.

The gull began to preen, pulling at her feathers, flattening and smoothing them as she worked.

"How come she does that?" asked Nick. "Looks like a girl who's all the time combing her hair."

Grandfather smiled. "Actually, it's a matter of life and death for a gull. See how it uses its bill? It's spreading oil over its feathers to waterproof them. Those feathers will keep it from getting wet or cold."

His words reminded Nick of what Kashi had said. "Kashi was telling me how wonderfully God designed the feathers on sea birds, with little barbs that sort of lock them together."

Grandfather changed the subject abruptly. "Looks like that bird's almost ready to be set free."

"I guess so. As soon as Kashi gets back, he'll probably say it's time." Nick sighed. "I know I can't keep her."

"Where'd your Japanese friend go?"

"He had a long flight this weekend." Nick gave Grandfather a sideways glance. "So he wasn't at the Tea after all."

The gull flew to another bedpost, left a dropping there, then flapped over to the window seat.

Nick stirred uneasily. "I'll clean that up and then maybe we'd better go. Mom will have a fit."

"Guess so," Grandfather said. "But thanks for bringing it over."

By the time Nick got back to the Inn, Robbie had come up from the beach. He'd rigged up two poles and had flown his kite while he was tending them. "You know what?" Robbie said. "I'd like to build another kite—a really big one. Kashi's supposed to be home tonight. How about if I phone and ask if we can come over tomorrow afternoon?"

"Sure," said Nick. Maybe he could make a star kite. He was still worried about Kashi, but he didn't want to say anything. "Did you check with Mom?"

"Yes, she'll need some extra help tomorrow morning for the party, but the afternoon's okay as long as we get back by 4:00."

"Another party?"

Robbie lowered his voice. "It's a big secret. Tina's having a surprise birthday party for her mother, tomorrow night. We're all supposed to come, but we can't talk about it."

"Oh, that's right." Nick groaned inside. "Do we have to bring presents?"

"Nah. Tina said it's the thought that counts. Mom doesn't even have to make a cake. Tina phoned this morning to say she's bringing a bunch of stuff from town. The food might be pretty good, at least."

"Guess so," Nick said. "Well, tell me what Kashi says about the kites." He retreated to his room. Even though he didn't feel like doing anything, he'd better work on his notebook.

He flipped restlessly through it and came to the page he had labeled "How Wings Fly." He had written only a couple of sentences, then he'd drawn a bunch of curly question marks in the margin. That was before he had some books to help him. Maybe now he could figure it out.

For a long time he read about wings and how they were constructed and how important they were for birds, but he couldn't find anything that explained how the wings actually made the birds fly. He stared out of his window, seeing nothing. Maybe there was some way he could get out of that party tomorrow.

Suddenly Nick remembered that Archie had promised to get back in time for it. Would he dare to come back if he'd stolen Mrs. McHugh's bracelet? Perhaps, if he'd found a way to get rid of it.

The next morning, Nick knew as soon as he came downstairs that Archie had returned. The little orange car was parked outside, and his typewriter was clattering busily. Even though Nick kept a careful watch, Archie didn't come out of his room the whole morning, and by the time Nick and Robbie left for Kashi's house in the afternoon, he still hadn't appeared.

Nick couldn't make up his mind about Archie. What did a guilty person look like, anyway? In the books he'd read, the hero just *knew* who it was, somehow.

On their way to Kashi's house, Nick told Robbie about finding the kittiwake and how Kashi was taking care of it. He didn't mind letting Robbie in on the secret now, since the kittiwake was doing better.

"Can I see it?" asked Robbie.

"Sure. Let's ask Kashi if we can do that first."

Kashi went out to the shed with them. "I took the screen off the box so it can move around freely and strengthen its wings."

The kittiwake flew out of her box when they stepped into the shed. She lighted on the workbench and eyed them expectantly. She didn't seem to mind when Kashi stepped close. He picked up a large feather and began stroking the bird's sleek white throat. "I try not to handle it anymore," he said, "because the oil on my hands could interfere with the natural waterproofing on its feathers." Nick tried to remember whether he'd touched her feathers very much yesterday. No, he'd mostly kept her in the towel.

"Ready for a bite to eat?" Kashi said to the bird. He tossed a kernel of corn into the air and the gull leaned over, catching it effortlessly. Kashi smiled at Nick and Robbie. "Here, want to try?"

They took turns throwing grain for the bird to catch until she walked a few steps away from them and began preening her feathers. Kashi glanced at Nick. "That wing is plenty strong now. It's time to let the bird go."

He was right, Nick had to admit. They walked over to Kashi's house, and on the way he asked, "When?"

"How about tomorrow afternoon?"

"Okay." He'd get one more chance to see her. And he'd better not stroke her feathers then, either.

Nick pulled his thoughts away from the kittiwake and tried to concentrate on his new kite. Kashi showed him how to tie the bamboo sticks into the right shape, then he framed them with string while Kashi and Robbie planned the giant kite.

When they started talking about the giant kites used for kite festivals in Japan, Nick asked about the fighting kites Grandfather had mentioned.

Kashi chuckled. "Yes, that is a sight to see, my grandfather told me. *Hata* kites. They've got a very long bridle, and at the end of the bridle there's about twenty feet of line coated with a paste they make from ground-up glass. That's the cutting line."

"How can they get close enough to cut down each other's kites?" asked Nick.

"The flyer is very skilled—he makes his kite dip and turn in just the right way so he can saw through the other kite's main line," said Kashi. "Those *hata* kites are amazingly agile."

"I'd sure like to make one some day," said Robbie.

Not me, thought Nick. I want to make a bird kite like Kashi's hawk, with real feathers and everything.

As Kashi and Robbie set to work, he turned back to his star kite. He'd decorate it with the outline of a flying kittiwake. He practiced some designs on scrap paper and experimented with Kashi's paints, then he chose his best design and painted it onto the kite. He was adding black to the bird's wingtips when Robbie asked casually, "Do you know whether Mrs. McHugh got her bracelet back yet?"

"I don't think she did." Nick gripped the paintbrush tightly and held his breath to make it stop wobbling. Silently he finished the second wing, not daring to look at Kashi.

"Mrs. McHugh is usually a wise person," said Kashi in his deep, calm voice, "but this time I think she's mistaken. Rob, make sure you get that frame perfectly symmetrical. And you'll need an extra long bridle."

He chose a ball of kite string and handed it to Robbie. "You boys coming to the birthday party tonight? Tina is just like her mother—she does excellent parties."

Nick was glad when Robbie took up the conversation, telling about all the preparations that had been made. While his brother talked, he kept busy with the streamers for his kite. At least now he could stop worrying about what Kashi thought. But he still didn't want to go to that party.

By the time they got back to the Inn, Tina was bustling around in the kitchen. She said her mother was taking a walk on the beach. The food was all ready, including a tall cake shaped like a castle. She sent Nick up to Grandfather with a hand-written invitation to the party.

"Not me." Grandfather slid down into the sheets as if he were afraid she'd drag him out. "No way I'm going to go down there for the McDragon's birthday."

Nick couldn't blame him. "Me neither," he said. "I sure don't want to go."

Grandfather was silent, and Nick felt the black eyes studying him. At last Grandfather sighed. "Nick, you'd better go."

"How come?"

"Just to prove that you're innocent. A guilty person wouldn't show up for something like that."

"But she makes me *feel* guilty," Nick protested. "Just the way she looks at me."

"I know what you mean."

Grandfather didn't say anything more. Nick wandered over to the window seat and sat down on it with a thump. "Okay, I guess I'll go, if you think I should. I just hope they don't have any stupid games."

Somehow Tina and Mom managed to have everything ready by the time Mrs. McHugh returned. The two friends from town arrived at the same time Kashi did, and Archie wandered out of his room at the last minute, looking dazed. Mrs. McHugh had gone into her bedroom to change clothes for supper. As soon as she came out, Tina began to sing "Happy Birthday to You" and everyone joined in. "Surprise!" she cried, hugging her mother.

Mrs. McHugh looked embarrassed, not surprised, Nick thought. But probably, with a daughter like Tina, she'd stopped being surprised years ago.

They all sat at one long table in the dining room, except Robbie and Nick, who acted as waiters. That suited Nick fine. He could eat in the kitchen and enjoy the food without everyone staring at him. By now, Tina must have heard about the bracelet, and Archie too. He hadn't decided yet whether Archie looked guilty; he'd have to wait until the dreamy expression wore off his face. Archie's hair had changed to a more natural color, though.

After the meal, Tina ushered everyone into Mrs. McHugh's parlor, which she had decorated lavishly with green crepe paper and balloons. Nick made sure he got a chair by the door. Mrs. McHugh hadn't seemed to notice that he was there. Good. Maybe he could leave pretty soon. There was plenty to do in the kitchen, anyway.

"First the presents, then the cake," Tina declared. She handed around clear glass cups of pink punch, and seemed to be bursting with excitement. "Here's the first one." She picked up a square white box and passed it to her mother.

"Why, Archie, how nice!" Mrs. McHugh smiled and held up a bright blue mug that said *Woods Hole* on both sides.

Kashi's present was a slim book of poems, bound in red leather. Nick was glad to see that there was a gift from Mom and him and Robbie. It turned out to be a kit for drying and pressing flowers. Mrs. McHugh looked pleased with that.

Tina turned to her mother. "There's one or two more gifts," she said, her eyes gleaming. "This first one isn't anything actually *new,* but I thought you would enjoy your Sunday tea parties more if you had it to wear." She handed her mother a small rectangular box.

Mrs. McHugh darted a curious glance at her daughter and unwrapped it swiftly. "Oh!" She turned pale under the rouge on her old cheeks. "Oh, my." She clutched at the table as if she were going to faint.

Nick craned his neck to see what it was.

Tina leaned forward and took a bracelet from the box. It was gold, set with pearls and purple stones. He waited, tingling.

Tina explained. "You've all seen this, I'm sure. It's Mother's favorite bracelet that I gave her years ago. Recently she broke the clasp on it, so I smuggled it out and got it fixed." She gave her mother a worried glance. "I can't imagine what's the—"

"Tina, sit down for a minute, please." Mrs. McHugh took a deep breath and seemed to regain her composure. She looked straight at Nick. "There you are, Nicholas. It was so kind of you to come today, in spite of . . ." Her voice shook, then steadied. "My dear lad, I have wronged you terribly. I am so sorry. Please forgive me."

She faced her daughter. "Tina, last week I looked and looked for the bracelet and finally concluded that it had been stolen. And I was foolish enough to—to—accuse Nicholas of taking it. Oh, I am *so* sorry!"

She took the bracelet from Tina and bent her head to put it on, fumbling with the clasp. Kashi jumped up to help her. Archie tried to get there first and succeeded only in dropping his cup and saucer, which clattered to the rug.

"Thank you, Mr. Yoshimura," she murmured. She sent Nick an agonized glance. "My Malcolm always said, 'Be sure to question every possible witness.' If only I'd followed his advice!" She shook her head, then she turned her attention back to the party. "Thank you, Archie, for such a gallant attempt." Everyone chuckled, and she smiled at Tina. "That was a very thoughtful gift, my dear."

Tina smiled back, only a little subdued.

The next present was a book about Scottish castles, and then there was a puzzle: a three-dimensional model of a castle to be constructed with interlocking pieces. Nick sat without moving, letting the party swirl around him, conscious only of bubbling happiness inside.

At last Tina brought out the castle cake, and everyone sang "Happy Birthday" once more. While Nick was hoping that the cake would be chocolate, he noticed a green envelope poking out of the castle tower.

"And what is this?" Mrs. McHugh said, opening it. She pulled out something that looked like tickets. "Tina, what have you done?"

Tina rushed over and linked arms with her mother. "We're going on a trip, mother dear. To Scotland! To explore castles!"

Mrs. McHugh looked amazed, and Tina beamed. Kashi began clapping, then everyone joined in.

Mrs. McHugh finally cut the cake, and Tina passed it around while the grownups drank coffee and talked about the trip to Scotland. It sounded as though Tina and her mother were going to leave tomorrow afternoon. Nick helped himself to another piece of cake, since it had turned out to be chocolate, and fixed a plate for Grandfather. Whistling softly, he stopped in the kitchen to fill a Thermos with the special chocolate-flavored coffee Tina had made. Then he hurried up the stairs.

13

Hang in There

Grandfather looked as though he'd been expecting him. "I thought you might be all partied out by now."

Nick told him what had happened, and for once Grandfather listened without interrupting. "Well," he said at last, "she's a real lady, to apologize to you in front of everyone like that. I'm glad it turned out well for you, Nick. Sometimes you get accused of something and no one ever finds out the truth. Reminds me of a fellow I knew—"

Nick settled at the foot of the bed to listen, nibbling at his cake from time to time.

Later, in bed that night, he thought about the story Grandfather had told. What if something else had happened to that bracelet and no one ever found it? The Lord had been good to him, letting it turn out this way. And ever since the night he'd talked to the Lord about Mrs. McHugh, he'd started feeling different about her. After what happened today, she seemed more like a real person—someone who could even make a mistake. Just like he'd made, suspecting Archie.

The next morning, Nick wondered how he could've thought Archie might steal the bracelet. There was obviously just one thing on Archie's mind, and that was his book. Now that he had decided on an underwater world for his people, he talked nonstop about it.

"See, it's a community of very intelligent creatures. I call it Pelagia," he told Nick. "They have clear bodies, like jellyfish, and tentacles that can do almost anything." Robbie asked him whether he had seen any flounder at Woods Hole, and then they talked for a long time while Robbie was supposed to be mopping the kitchen floor.

Nick had almost finished dusting when he heard Archie say, "There's a good-sized aquarium near here. I'm going down there tomorrow—it's only a couple of hours' drive. I'll stay overnight and come back the next day. Hey, Rob, why don't we ask your mother if you can go with me?"

They hurried off upstairs, and Nick felt like trailing after them, saying, "Me, too?" He swished his dust cloth over the mantel. Maybe it wasn't such a good idea for him to go along, anyway. Mom needed him here, and he was beginning to think that Grandfather might miss him.

Archie and Robbie clattered back downstairs, making plans to leave early the next morning. Robbie grabbed the mop. "I've got to finish this up so I can pack." He disappeared into the kitchen, then called to Nick, "Mom said to put those library books on the kitchen table for Mrs. McHugh to take back." A minute later, he asked, "We still going to fly our kites this afternoon? Hope the weather holds."

Nick had been checking the sky every once in a while. It was covered with lumpy-looking clouds, but the breeze was still light. More important, this was the day for setting the kittiwake free.

That afternoon the wind picked up, but Robbie didn't think it would be too strong for kites, so they took them along. Nick showed him the shortcut to Kashi's house, and on the way they talked about letting the kittiwake go. "I wonder what Kashi will do," Nick said.

"Maybe just take the box outside and see what happens."

"I hope he takes the kittiwake down to the beach so she'll feel more at home," said Nick.

Kashi was already in the shed when they arrived. It looked as though the gull had done a lot of flying already, judging from the feathers scattered about. Nick picked up a white one and a gray one that was tipped with black. He'd tape them into his gull notebook.

"Ready?" asked Kashi. "Let's get this bird back into the air."

He wrapped a towel around the gull and tucked it under one arm. "Why don't we go down to the beach?"

Nick walked right behind Kashi so he could keep an eye on the kittiwake. She observed everything with bright eyes, offering no resistance until they left the shelter of the bushes. Once on the beach, with the waves lapping nearby and the salty wind streaming past, she began to struggle.

"Okay, I know what you want," said Kashi. Near the water's edge, he knelt and gently unwrapped the bird. She took a few steps, leaving flowerlike tracks in the sand, and shook her feathers into place. Then she took off into the wind, rising almost straight up, her wings beating powerfully in perfect unison. She wheeled, ignoring the other gulls, and flew directly toward the gray clouds on the horizon.

Nick watched until she became a white speck and vanished into the clouds. He'd sort of hoped she would circle back, maybe swooping low in a last farewell, like birds always did in films.

Kashi chuckled. "Looks like our kittiwake had an appointment to keep and didn't want to be late."

"You guys probably saved its life," said Robbie.

Nick smiled then. That was a good thing to remember. He took a careful look at the tracks in the sand and decided he could sketch them for his notebook. "C'mon," said Robbie. "Let's get these kites into the air too."

That evening, while Grandfather stumped up and down on his crutches, Nick told him about flying the new kites.

"Robbie's was so big that Kashi had to hold it up for him while he ran down the beach. And even then it took a while to get launched. My star kite flew just fine, all by itself."

He paused, remembering how his kite had looked like a bird, a flicker of white, dancing against the clouds. That reminded him. "We let the kittiwake go today. She flew straight out to sea." He stopped at the window and pulled back the drapes, but he could see only his reflection in the glass.

"I asked Kashi where she would go. He said she'd probably join a flock somewhere, maybe a few miles out from shore." Nick pictured a cloud of kittiwakes whirling above the water. "Isn't it amazing about the kittiwakes, how they actually live out over the ocean? Just think about all the different kinds of gulls the Lord made. Kashi says—"

"That's enough!" Grandfather dropped one crutch beside the bed and stood there, swaying, his face dark with anger. "I've heard plenty about what Kashi says."

Nick felt as if he'd been hit in the stomach. "How come you don't like him? Just because he's Japanese . . ."

"No, that's not it." Grandfather sat heavily on the bed. "I knew lots of Japanese when I was stationed there, and most of them were okay." He grunted. "But there was one, a short man with a round, smiling face, always smiling, smiling. He talked about God all the time—he kept saying that God loved me and Christ died for my sins—he quoted Bible verses every time I turned around. That's who your Takashi Yoshimura reminds me of, and I'm sick of it."

He hoisted his legs onto the bed. "I don't need God. I don't need anybody. You can hate me for being a grouchy old man, but just leave me alone." He snatched up his earphones and clamped them on.

Nick stared at him. He wanted to sit down, to think of a careful answer, but there was no time; indignant words rose in his mind and boiled out. "I'm just a kid, but I know I need God. The Japanese guy was right—God does love you. He can change you from being a grouchy old man. He changed me. He's still changing me—that's why I don't hate Mrs. McHugh anymore. And—and—"

His throat closed; he had to stop. Was Grandfather listening? Maybe. The black eyes glittered at him from under the baseball cap.

He rushed from the room and was all the way down to the kitchen before he remembered Grandfather's tray. Let it stay there. He wasn't going back tonight.

His mother asked him about the tray, as he knew she would. "I forgot it," he said. "Grandfather got mad at me and I just . . . Mom, he's impossible. Here we've been praying all this time and nothing's happened. He said that Kashi reminds him of some guy in Japan who's a Christian. That's why he can't stand Kashi; he'll never listen to him. I tried saying something about the Lord, but he probably didn't hear me." Nick fell into a chair and covered his face with his hands.

His mother came to put an arm around him. "I know, Nicky; it breaks my heart. He used to stamp out of the room whenever your father witnessed to him. But hang in there. God's going to do this *His* way." She squeezed his shoulder. "You've made a good start. I think your grandfather is truly fond of you."

"Thanks, Mom." He sighed. "Kashi warned me about getting discouraged." Automatically he began helping with the dishes, and the evening slid by with its usual routines. But the sadness in his grandfather's eyes haunted him until at last he fell asleep.

During the night, an off-sea wind arose, and by dawn it blew around the house in great roaring gusts. The tree outside Nick's window tossed and rattled its branches until he finally got up and shut his window against the noise. When he woke again, the wind was still blowing hard, and rain sluiced down the windowpanes.

Why was everybody being so quiet, he wondered on his way down to breakfast. Then he remembered. Yesterday afternoon, Mrs. McHugh and Tina had gone to the airport, and Archie and Robbie had left early this morning. The Inn was almost empty.

Grandfather wasn't very talkative, even though Mom had made apple walnut pancakes. Nick opened the drapes and gazed out at the dark, scudding clouds. A pair of black-backed gulls flew past, beating hard into the wind. "Looks like we're having quite a storm," Nick said. He stayed to watch the gulls veer sideways across the wind and sweep into a long descending spiral that took them out of sight.

Grandfather muttered something from the bed, and Nick thought about what he'd said the night before: *I don't need anybody.*

He needs a friend, Nick thought for the hundredth time. A friend like Kashi. Silently he prayed, "Lord, what can I do to help Grandfather? He needs You most of all."

He walked past the bed, thinking that he might as well leave. Grandfather spoke through a mouthful of pancake. "How's the sea gull notebook coming along?"

Nick thought back to the last time he'd worked on it. "Well, there's one part that's got me kind of stumped," he said. "I was trying to explain how birds fly, you know—how those sea gulls can just take off like they do—and I guess I don't really understand how it works."

"The theory of flight, huh?" Grandfather put down his fork. "Okay, it's the same with a bird or an airplane. The airplane moves forward, and because of the shape of its wings, there's more air pressure under the wing than above it."

"How come?" asked Nick.

"That's because the air can move faster over the top of the wing. Here, let me show you."

Grandfather picked up a pencil and drew on his paper napkin. "See, here's an airplane wing. As the airplane starts moving, the air coming at it curves up quickly over the top of the wing and more slowly underneath. So the air pressure builds up under the wing, pushes it up, and then lifts the airplane." He put down his pencil. "Just remember that high air pressure under the wing lifts it up."

"The same for a kite?" asked Nick.

"Yes siree, you've got it!" exclaimed Grandfather. "Even if the kite doesn't have a curved surface on top, it lies at an angle to the wind. The movement of air makes a high pressure area and pushes it up, so it flies."

He handed the napkin to Nick. "Thanks," said Nick. "That helps a lot." He picked up Grandfather's breakfast tray, then he had to put it down to add last night's dishes. He could feel the old man watching him.

Grandfather let out a long breath that might have been a sigh. "Nick, I'm sorry about last night." He frowned. "You sounded like your father, standing there, talking about God." The corners of his mouth turned down. "I've fought against God for a long time. I doubt very much that He loves me—if He ever did."

Nick opened his mouth to protest, and Grandfather put up a hand. "No, let it be, Nick. I don't want to fight with you. Now it's time for me to get dressed, and I'm sure your mother is wondering where those dishes are. Tell her I liked the pancakes."

Silently Nick left the room, not sure what to think. At least Grandfather didn't seem angry any more.

Mom had plans for a cooking project, and he helped her chop vegetables for a huge pot of soup instead of doing chores. Every once in a while he made a quick trip to the living room windows to check on the storm.

Lightning flickered, far out at the horizon where masses of dark clouds seemed to rise from the water. The sea had turned olive green, and mountainous foam-crested waves raced wildly for shore. Rank after rank they came, booming as they crashed onto the small beach below. They sounded awfully close, Nick thought.

At lunch time, the storm still howled outside, and rain beat against the kitchen windows. Definitely a day to stay inside. While Grandfather took his nap, Nick decided to start on his page that described how birds fly. What had Grandfather called it? The theory of flight. That would make a good title.

He collected his books and made himself comfortable on the bed; the cat was already curled up, waiting for him. He glanced at the dark sky outside, and then he turned on the lamp.

He was adding some colorful arrows to his copy of Grandfather's drawing when thunder exploded outside his window. The cat sprang up and disappeared. Glaring white filled the room, thunder rolled again, the lights went out. Something slammed against the house, and the floor shuddered under his feet.

Nick leaped to the window as more lightning sheeted across the sky. Half the tree was gone. Huge branches lay embedded in the crumpled roof below—the kitchen roof.

He rushed into the dark hall. Where were the stairs?

Step by step, he felt his way down, frantic at the delay. "Mom?" he shouted into the darkness. He strained to hear an answer above the raging of the storm.

14
Careful!

At the next flash of lightning, Nick leaped down the rest of the stairs and into the kitchen.

Why was it so cold in here?

"Mom!"

He had to get a flashlight. In the drawer. He groped along the kitchen counter, yanked the drawer open, and fumbled for a flashlight. Finally he got it turned on. The first thing he saw was a ragged hole in the ceiling. A wide, shadowy mass of wood and plaster hung down from the hole. He sent the light down to where the wreckage met the floor. "Mom?" he whispered.

She lay on one side with her eyes closed; her legs were hidden under the pile of debris. He knelt and put a hand to her face. It felt cold and wet—was she breathing? Yes. He looked up at the rain spattering into her face and ran for an umbrella from the hall closet. Hurriedly he pulled two chairs over to prop up the umbrella, then stopped to stare again at the fallen wood and plaster. Had to get that stuff away from her, somehow.

He pulled experimentally at a piece of wood in the pile. Nothing moved. He pulled harder and something shifted, but plaster fragments showered onto his hair and face from above. Wait. Even if he could move it, he might bring the whole ceiling down on their heads.

He backed away from the dripping rain, and a whisper of panic rose inside him. Another thought sliced through his mind. What about Grandfather? His room was on the same side of the house as this. Was he okay?

Flashlight in hand, he took the stairs two at a time. He burst into the room and found the old man sitting straight up in bed. "What's happened?" asked Grandfather.

"It's Mom." Nick fought the quaver in his voice. "Part of the ceiling fell on her in the kitchen—from the tree. The storm—"

"Is she okay?"

"Yes—well, she's breathing but she's unconscious. Her legs are stuck and I can't move it without—"

"You'll have to get some help." Above the clamor of the storm, Grandfather's voice was calm, reasonable; it steadied Nick. "Phone Kashi. Get him to call for an ambulance. Then ask if he's got a jack we can borrow."

"Okay." Nick ran down to phone from the kitchen. Robbie had scribbled the number somewhere on the calendar. There it was.

Halfway through dialing, he realized that the phone was dead. The phone lines must be down too. He took another look at his mother and rushed back upstairs. "Phone is dead. I'll have to get Kashi. Be right back."

"Be careful, Nick." Grandfather's voice reached out to him through the darkness. He grabbed his jacket and a minute later was out the front door.

The wind slammed icy pellets of rain into his face as he ran down the steps to the beach, and he wished he'd thought to wear a slicker. The tide was high—higher than he'd ever seen it—and huge dark waves broke uncomfortably near. The surf thundered in his ears, shutting out everything else. He found only a narrow strip of sand for his feet, and he hadn't gone a dozen yards before it disappeared altogether. Swirling, boiling, foaming water swept around the dunes and ragged grasses: the beach was gone.

He turned back. The wind tore at him, snatching his breath away. He licked the salt spray off his lips, and it tasted bitter. What if Mom was bleeding? Why hadn't he checked? "Lord," he prayed, "what should I do?"

There had to be another way. What about his shortcut? He put his head down and threw himself into the wall of wind, back along the beach, up the steps; then he circled around the Inn. He flicked on the flashlight. It sent a pale, wavering light through the curtain of rain, but it was enough to show him the path.

Here the tall bushes cut the force of the wind, and he could breathe more easily. He ran as fast as he dared, keeping his eyes on the pale ribbon of sand that snaked into the darkness. Suddenly the ground was crumbling under his feet. He was sliding off it into water. A muddy river appeared in the beam of his flashlight—the gully had become a raging torrent.

He skidded to a halt and stepped back, panting. He could reach that island of grass with one big jump. Then another couple of jumps and he could get back to the path.

The water sloshed through his sneakers and splattered up his legs as he landed, but he made the first jump without falling in—the next three jumps too—and at last the path turned away from the gully.

Hurry—hurry, his pounding feet seemed to say. He wanted to run faster, but his breath came in painful gasps, slowing him.

Was this the clump of grass where he should turn? The storm had ripped away his marker; the feathery plumes looked thin and ragged, torn by the wind. This had to be it.

Turn here. Would Kashi be home? He didn't even know for sure.

He stumbled through the wildly tossing bushes, his feet and hands icy. Cold rain trickled down the back of his neck and dripped from his hair. He shook the water from his eyes. Soon, if this was the right way . . . Yes, he could see the weathervane gleaming through the dusk.

Lightning cracked—a blinding stroke that shook the earth—and he jumped aside in terror. Too close!

He clenched his teeth and kept on. Just a little farther . . .

He fixed his eyes on the light that shone from Kashi's house. One last effort, and he flung himself against the door.

After an endless moment, it opened. He fell inside, picked himself up, and looked into Kashi's startled face. Still gasping for breath, he delivered his message.

" . . . an ambulance, Grandfather said. And bring a jack."

"Right." Kashi made the phone call, pulling on a slicker as he talked. "Here—put something dry on your feet." He handed thick socks and a pair of boots to Nick.

He had trouble getting them on because of his stiff fingers, but they felt good and warm. "Here's another flashlight," Kashi said. "And we'll take a crowbar too. Can you carry it?"

"Sure."

"Okay. Jump into my car and I'll be right there."

Nick had forgotten about Kashi's old yellow station wagon. At least he didn't have to go back on that path.

As they bounced down a rutted, sandy road, Nick told Kashi how he had tried to move the pile of debris off his mother.

Kashi shook his head. "Good thing you stopped. Anyway, the beams they used for building those old houses are incredibly heavy."

They turned into the long driveway that led to the Inn. "Do you think the back door is blocked?" asked Kashi.

"Yes, I had to go out the front way."

The wind felt colder than ever, and the crowbar was icy in Nick's hands, but he kept up with Kashi's long stride. Hunched low against the gale, they rounded the corner of the Inn and sprinted up the veranda steps.

Kashi pulled the front door open, then shut it quickly behind them, and the wind dropped to a muffled roar. The hall was quiet and dark. Had someone closed the door to the kitchen?

Kashi turned on his flashlight, and they followed its beam to the kitchen. Cold, wet air rushed at them as Kashi opened the door. A large flashlight stood on the counter, and dripping rain glinted briefly in its dim light.

Nick rushed past the wreckage to where he had left his mother. Grandfather sat there on the floor beside her, his cast sticking out awkwardly in front. Nick could have hugged him.

His mother lay motionless, her eyes closed. Grandfather had covered her with the quilt from his bed, and the umbrella still protected her face. He glanced up at them and nodded to Kashi. "She's stabilized," he said calmly. "No bleeding that I can see. Looks like she hit her head when she fell."

"Okay," said Kashi. "We've got an ambulance on the way. Probably take them a while, this far out." He knelt beside Nick's mother and checked her pulse, then he stood up to study the wreckage.

Nick couldn't take his eyes off his mother's face. She looks too peaceful, he thought. She looks like someone who's . . . dead. He jerked himself around to watch Kashi.

"Let's see what we can do," Kashi was saying. He set up the jack beside the pile of wood and plaster. Then he stopped and eyed the ragged hole in the ceiling. "What do you think?"

he asked Grandfather. "Is the rest of it going to come down on her?"

"Could be," Grandfather said. He glanced around the shadowy kitchen. "How about using that table for a shield?"

"Good idea." Kashi moved swiftly to one end of the table. "Come on, Nick; we could use a little muscle."

As soon as Grandfather had taken down the umbrella and crawled out of the way, they positioned the table over Mom's head.

"Now I need you over here, Nick." Kashi braced the crowbar against the pile. "Hold onto this; we want to keep it from coming off the jack." He attached the lever to the jack. "Ready?"

Nick leaned against the crowbar with all his strength and stared at the fallen beams in front of him, willing them to move.

Kashi worked the jack, and the pile rose slowly. An inch of space widened to two, then three. "Good work. Keep it steady for me, Nick," said Kashi.

When the pile had been lifted about a foot off the floor, he stopped. "Won't go much higher."

Nick wanted to dash over and pull his mother away.

"Wait, Nick," said Grandfather, as if he could read his thoughts. "Hang onto that crowbar—we're depending on you." He was back under the table, checking Mom's pulse.

"I hate to move her," said Kashi, "but that stuff is getting wetter every minute."

"Maybe if we just take it easy—" began Grandfather.

"Wait!" exclaimed Nick. High above the sound of wind and rain came the thin wail of a siren.

"Good ears," said Kashi. He joined Nick at the crowbar. "I'll take care of this. Why don't you run outside and show them where to come in?"

It was a relief to do something, even to fight through the storm and around the corner of the Inn. The ambulance had already pulled up to the back door. "Over here," he called.

A minute later, the two attendants followed him inside, carrying their equipment and a stretcher. He dashed ahead of them, opening doors, wondering what they would say about Mom.

By the time he got the kitchen door closed, they were bending over his mother, asking questions and examining her legs. Nick hurried over to see how she was doing.

Her eyes were open. She smiled at him, and the tightness in his chest eased a little.

"We'll take her in," said one of the men. "Get a doctor to check her over." He gave Nick a kind glance. "She's going to be okay—don't worry."

"Can I go too?" he asked.

Kashi nodded. "We'll follow them in my car. I need to get in touch with Peter so he can take care of the roof. And something has to be done about the phone and electric wires."

They both looked at Grandfather.

"Don't worry about me." He gave Nick a sharp glance. "You'd better run upstairs and put on some dry clothes, or your mother'll have my scalp."

Nick clumped upstairs in the heavy boots and changed clothes faster than he ever had in his life. He shoved his feet into an old pair of sneakers and rushed back down.

His mother was in the ambulance. Kashi had lowered the pile of debris down to the floor. "That's a pretty big chunk to keep up in the air," he said. "Safer on the floor. C'mon, let's go."

15
Yes Siree

On the way to the hospital, the rain seemed to slacken. "Maybe the storm's blowing itself out," Kashi said.

Nick thought about Grandfather, alone in the old house, and he hoped so.

They drove around the back of a tall brick hospital to where a lighted sign said EMERGENCY. The ambulance was parked there, empty.

"They've got her inside already," said Kashi. "A doctor's probably looking after her right now."

He didn't jump out of the car as Nick had expected. "Want to pray together?" asked Kashi.

Nick nodded, and Kashi prayed aloud. He thanked God for His loving care, then he prayed for Nick's mother and for the doctor and for the repair of the house. He paused. "And Father, please use this to somehow reach the grandfather's heart. Use us to show him Your love and to speak of You."

Silently Nick echoed Kashi's prayer. "Yes, Lord, please."

After he'd finished, Kashi said, "Your grandfather's a remarkable man, Nick."

He wanted to smile at that. Kashi hadn't seen Grandfather in one of his tempers.

"Let's go find the waiting room," Kashi said. "They'll have a pay phone I can use. For one thing, I need to talk to the telephone repair people."

While Kashi filled out some papers and made his phone calls, Nick waited, flipping through magazines and making trips to the drinking fountain. The room was crowded, mostly with older people. Once an ambulance brought in someone who was immediately whisked down the long hallway.

He fidgeted in the hard wooden chair. What if Mom's legs were broken? What if she was going to be crippled? What if—he stopped himself, remembering Kashi's confidence in God's care.

Kashi returned, and finally a nurse called them up to the desk. A doctor spoke to them. "She's got a bump on her head and some bruises, but she'll be okay in a couple of days," he said. "We'd like to keep her overnight, just to make sure."

"Oh!" exclaimed Nick, "where is she? Can I talk to her?"

The doctor shook his head wearily, but his voice was kind. "She's resting. She said to tell you she's all right. Think you can wait until tomorrow?"

"Guess so." Nick looked at Kashi.

Kashi smiled. "Thank you, doctor; that's good news." Then he asked what time they could come for her. Nick was grateful to him.

Back in the car, Kashi told him that Peter would be out with a crew of men early the next morning to work on the roof. "Hey, are you hungry?" he asked. "Does the grandfather like pizza?"

"He loves it," Nick said. He felt suddenly comforted by Kashi's thinking of ordinary things like food. "Can we take him some?"

"You said it."

Nick grinned in the darkness. "More coals of fire?"

"Supper for a hungry friend," Kashi said.

At the pizza shop they picked up sodas and a large double supreme pizza, and Kashi talked the owner into letting them borrow an insulated carrier to keep it hot. By the time they reached the Inn, the rain had stopped and a few stars blinked overhead. "Good thing," Kashi remarked, looking up at the thinning clouds. "Peter was going to come out tonight if the rain kept on."

They found Grandfather upstairs in his room, looking smug. "Latched onto a Coleman stove and made me some good hot coffee," he said. He'd set up the stove on the bureau and lighted half a dozen candles.

"What?" he exclaimed when he saw what Kashi was carrying. "Pizza? I must be in heaven."

Nick flinched. But Kashi grinned and said, "No way. And we're not angels, either. We're starving." He paused and smiled at them both. "Let's thank the Lord for this good food." He bowed his head over the box of pizza and asked a short blessing.

To Nick's relief, Grandfather sat quietly.

"Okay, Nick, bring on those sodas," said Kashi, "and let the party begin."

This was a good idea, Nick thought, as he bit into his second piece of pizza. Grandfather and Kashi had talked about Mom, and about the storm, and about Peter coming to fix the roof. Then they began swapping airplane stories. They seemed to be getting along. Grandfather was talking more than Nick had ever thought he could.

Now he had switched to football. "I'll tell you right now, I'm a Giants fan. Always have been. How about that game tomorrow! The Giants are really going to clean up." Grandfather settled back with a half-eaten piece of pizza.

Kashi raised an eyebrow. "Well now, I wouldn't be too sure about that."

Grandfather leaned forward, staring at him. "What d'you mean?"

"The third Super Bowl—that's what the Colts thought when they played against the Jets. And lo and behold, Joe Namath picked their secondary apart."

"But we're not talking about the Colts and the Jets. This is the *Giants!*"

"Maybe so, but they'd better remember that they're going to face a jelling defense and an up-and-coming young quarterback who throws a lot like Joe Namath."

Kashi had a quirk to his mouth that meant he was teasing. But he shouldn't be teasing Grandfather about his favorite team, Nick thought. Grandfather was going to be furious.

"I'm telling you, the Giants have a great quarterback." Grandfather's eyes glittered angrily.

"Well, you're certainly entitled to your opinion," Kashi said, looking unperturbed. "But I don't think their defense has been working together lately. I guess we'll just see what happens at that game tomorrow."

Grandfather glared at Kashi. Hurriedly Nick asked, "I've been wondering, Grandfather—how did you ever get downstairs all by yourself this afternoon?"

Grandfather glared at him instead. "You don't think I've been stumping around up here all this time for nothing, do you? The doctor said this is a walking cast, and I can tell you, I've had it with crutches. You'd have laughed to see me getting down those stairs on the seat of my pants. But this leg is getting stronger every day. Have you got any more soda?"

Nick brought him another can while Kashi sat quietly, his brown eyes gleaming. Grandfather took a long drink and slanted a glance at Kashi. "Nice to run into someone who knows something about football. That's sure going to be some game tomorrow. Hope the electricity's back on by then."

"Well, there's nothing wrong with my TV set." Kashi stood up. "Pizza's all gone, Nick. Looks like we'd better do the dishes."

Reluctantly Nick helped him gather napkins and soda cans into the pizza box. He carried it downstairs and then decided he'd better take it to the outside trash can. When he returned, Grandfather was chuckling at something, and Kashi was saying good night.

Nick accompanied Kashi down the stairs. He almost tripped over the cats, who were waiting hungrily. After Kashi had driven off, he fed the cats and went back upstairs to see Grandfather. He had changed into pajamas and was brushing his teeth in the tiny bathroom. He finished, then hobbled back to his bed and sat down with a long drawn-out sigh. "What a day."

He looked exhausted, Nick thought. The flickering candlelight shadowed his face and made it look thinner than ever. But his eyes weren't angry anymore.

Grandfather leaned against the pillows. "That friend of yours—he's okay," he said drowsily. "He's coming back tomorrow. Or I might go over there to see the game. See his kites. Maybe ask him about those fighting kites."

Nick wanted to explain what he'd learned about the *hata* kites, then he decided not to. Let him talk to Kashi.

"Don't worry about your mother, okay?" Grandfather slid down under the blankets. "And would you please blow out the candles?" He grinned. "Sleep well, my boy. Yes siree—you've certainly earned it."

He left the dark room with Grandfather's words of praise glowing inside him. He switched on his flashlight and headed for the stairs. Somewhere, a phone began to ring.

They've fixed the lines, he thought.

Mom's room was the closest.

The phone rang and rang as he rushed down the steps, down the hall, and into her bedroom, knocking over a chair in the unfamiliar darkness. Finally he stumbled against her bedside table and grabbed the phone. "Hello?"

"Nicky, is that you?" His mother's voice was soft and warm.

"Aren't you asleep? How come . . ."

"When I woke up, the nurse let me call you—"

"How are you?" he said.

"I feel a little better. Just wanted to say hello and see if everything's all right."

"We're okay," said Nick. "We ate pizza with Grandfather, and he got along fine with Kashi."

"That's wonderful! The Lord's answering your prayers, Nicky."

Sounded like she was smiling from ear to ear. He wished he could see that.

"You're right, Mom. Hey, Kashi and I prayed for you. Sure your legs are okay?"

"Sure. They feel kind of stiff, but the doctor says they'll be good as new. Don't you worry. I'll see you tomorrow."

"Okay." Slowly he put down the phone. *Tomorrow.* The word soared through his mind, full of golden promise. Tomorrow she was coming home. Tomorrow Kashi was coming back—because Grandfather had asked him to.

He found the little striped cat waiting for him by his bedroom door. "I'm going to check on Grandfather," he said, thinking the phone might have wakened him. Near the top of the stairs, he stopped to yawn, and a furry shadow twined itself around his ankles. He scooped the cat up into his arms.

Light snoring sounded from Grandfather's room. He smiled and ruffled the cat's soft fur. "Tomorrow, Short Stuff," he whispered. "Yes siree."

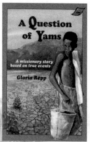